"Whether he was talking abo[illegible] drama of the American bran[illegible] California and the West, Jim [illegible] was a master at taking the fire that enlivens great storytelling from his own hea[illegible] and planting it in yours."

—Wallace Baine, author of *Rhymes with Vain*

"One of Jim's great gifts was to listen. I mostly ran into him only at Squaw Valley in the summers, so I saw him in times when he was happy and relaxed—though I would bet he was happy and relaxed pretty much all the time, wherever he was—but even on vacation there, he had a way of listening, and paying attention, with an intensity that generally cleared the air. Not only in conversation but in performing music too, his listening was a form of elegance. Behind the upright bass holding the rhythm steady, or strumming his very good, small, old guitar, he was always tuned in."

—Louis B. Jones, author of *Radiance*

"A splendid raconteur, Jim always put the story first—a story of restless people in motion, seeking opportunity, wealth, security, and redemption in regions new at least to themselves, receding ever westward. He loved the ease and warmth and freedom of life in Northern California[...and] his humor, optimism, and generosity of spirit were deeply rooted in this most favored of places. Emerging as it does from this richly mingled background, Jim's message to us is clear: love this place as you love your life in it, and preserve it for those who follow."

—Forrest Robinson, author of *Wallace Stegner*

"No matter how accomplished a novelist he was, [Jim Houston] was an even better man....All Jim's stories were passionately told and professionally crafted and absolutely honest. His novels consistently exhibited this gifted man working through his characters toward the truth of situations. He loved California and it loved him back."

—Gerald Haslam, co-editor with James D. Houston of *California Heartland: Writing from the Great Central Valley*

"James D. Houston wrote some of the finest fiction and essays set in the Far West and Pacific Rim. He had a westerly vision like a transcendent breeze bucking the prevailing easterlies in our literature, his eyes set square on the setting sun. A tender man, he wrote sensitively but often on an epic scale, knowing his characters, heroic and frail, like family and neighbors, imagining their sagas and intimate quirks. His fictive map traversed from edges of the Great Basin, over the Sierra Nevada to the Central Valley, and onto the Hawaiian Islands, where his last great novels are set. Jim was one of the most profound men in my life and a cherished heart. *No ka ipo lei manu...*"

—Garrett Hongo, author of *Coral Road*

"[Jim Houston was] deeply embedded...in this landscape and this community. Perceptive, generous, interested in everything and everyone[...]he was a fantastic writer and an even better human being."

—Karen Joy Fowler, author of *The Jane Austen Book Club*

"There was a quality of attention Jim Houston had, whether it was to the natural landscape in his work or the interior landscape of his characters. Few people I've known were so fully present the way Jim was, generous with his time and humor and affection. I miss that most about him, [and] am consoled by the books that retain so much of the man."

—Ehud Havazalet, author of *Bearing the Body*

"When I moved to Santa Cruz, Wallace Stegner said, 'Be sure to get to know the Houstons.' That was in the sixties, before Jim had published. Jeanne and Jim remained good friends from those early days. One of my fondest memories is of Jim bringing his bass to the annual Christmas party in Santa Cruz to provide music and good humor. The music of Hawaii had always drawn him, too, and he took delight in its sweet beauty, its surf and lore, and was moved by the tragic history of its people. How wonderful for his readers that Hawaii informs the last words from James D. Houston!"

—Charlotte Painter, author of *Conjuring Tibet*

"Jim helped me find my place in the stream of writers who've come of age in or passed through the Golden State. I think Jim had that effect on many people, many writers. Along with his books, that is his legacy—a pioneer's trail blazed from antique past to hyperbolic present, with plenty of stops to admire the view, smell the abalone on the grill, and sample the roadside attractions."

—Don Wallace, author of *Hot Water*

A QUEEN'S JOURNEY

Foreword by Alan Cheuse

Afterword by Maxine Hong Kingston

Heyday, Berkeley, California

Library of Congress Cataloging-in-Publication Data

Houston, James D.
A queen's journey / James D. Houston ; foreword by Alan Cheuse ; afterword by Maxine Hong Kingston.
p. cm.
ISBN 978-1-59714-163-5 (alk. paper)
1. Liliuokalani, Queen of Hawaii, 1838–1917--Fiction. 2. Journalists--Fiction. 3. Hawaii--History--19th century--Fiction. I. Title.
PS3558.O87Q44 2011
813'.54--dc22

2011025147

Book Design: Lorraine Rath
Printing and Binding: Thomson-Shore, Dexter, MI

Orders, inquiries, and correspondence should be addressed to:
Heyday
P.O. Box 9145, Berkeley, CA 94709
(510) 549-3564, Fax (510) 549-1889
www.heydaybooks.com

10 9 8 7 6 5 4 3 2 1

On receiving my full release I felt greatly inclined to go abroad, it made no difference where, as long as it would be a change.

—Lili'uokalani
In *Hawaii's Story by Hawaii's Queen*
(Boston, 1898)

This book is dedicated to the memory of Iolani Luahine, Nona Beamer, and Mornah Simeona.

Special thanks to Myrna Kamae, Pono Shim, Judith Flanders Staub, Alice Guild, and Mary Philpotts.

CONTENTS

FOREWORD

Alan Cheuse

"For people in their seventies," writes Nicholas Delbanco in *Lastingness,* his masterly study of great artists in their old age, "the future is a finite thing and what's extensive is tradition: the long reach of the past." As the esteemed and celebrated novelist and essayist James D. Houston, author of a number of highly lauded novels and essays on California life and Pacific Rim themes, approached his own mid-seventies, he must have felt that pinch and tightening of years that never afflicts the younger artist—we all do, we all will—but he was too deep into the research and note-making for the third in his trio of historical novels about California and the Pacific Rim to let it affect him.

In the first of these, *Snow Mountain Passage,* we traveled with the ill-fated Donner Party up into the Sierra Nevada in winter, some but not all of the characters—many based on historical figures with whom Houston felt an intimate relation—making it, at great physical and emotional cost, over the mountain passes to California. In *Bird of Another Heaven,* Houston reverses the direction of his characters' journey and gives us the voyage eastward from Hawai'i to San Francisco and beyond, as it was taken by the historical figure David Kalakaua, Hawaii's last king, and as narrated by the half-Hawaiian, half-indigenous California Indian woman who became his putative consort during the last days of his life.

For the third novel in this group, Houston envisioned an even broader geographical and political and social scheme. In *A Queen's Journey* he opens his arms to embrace a large swathe of historical and political time—from mid-nineteenth century Hawai'i on to Boston and Washington, D.C., just before the turn of the century.

Two figures lead the cast of mostly historical characters. First is Queen Lili'uokalani, the Royal Monarch deposed in the military coup arranged by the so-called Missionary Boys, the group of white businessmen, many of them descendants of the original missionaries who made landfall in Hawai'i in the 1820s. The second is the narrator, Julius, a New England journalist who has a deep affection for the queen and takes up the job of working on her behalf during her American sojourn.

Houston's research, as it was for his previous books, was painstaking and extensive. But as lovers of fine historical fiction know, and as any writer (including yours truly) who has attempted to create historical fiction can testify, historical narrative begins, rather than ends, with the facts. In Houston's case, as in the work of other contemporary creators of superb and deeply engaging historical fiction—such as Barry Unsworth's *Sacred Hunger,* a fine novel about the British slave trade, or Peter Matthiessen's *Shadow Country,* about the turn-of-the-century Florida wetlands renegade Tom Watson—the facts turn into the substance of a vision. In this inventive species of fiction the writer has to do all the work of an historian, and more. He has to gather his material meticulously, separate speculation from the actual acts of once-living men and women, imagine the context, the minutes, hours, days, and years, and the cities and weather experienced by his subjects. He has to feel the political and social context in his very skin and bones so that it becomes familiar enough that he does not over-explain in a way that people living in that time and place wouldn't do. Above all else, he has to spin the thread on which he strings every bead of fact, and then set it all ablaze with the flame and intensity of life itself so as to make a reader feel that he or she is watching just over the shoulder of the long-deceased historical actor.

So here is James Houston, embarking on this long journey—writing a short story is like, say, a canoe trip over a lake compared to the ocean voyage of a novel—with all of the usual enormous burdens of the novelist on his shoulders. And then comes along the ultimate burden, the cancer diagnosis that he wrestled with even as he began to wrestle with the new novel. We know he won the first round in that battle; these initial hundred pages, Part One of several projected sections, are finished in the best way, from the fiery intensity at the core of the narrative to the polish of every sentence.

The prologue, set on shipboard in Honolulu Harbor in 1868, sweeps us up into what we might first surmise to be an historical romance, when the narrator, New England journalist Julius, meets Lydia Dominis, a married Hawaiian woman with eyes "lit by black fire" who will before the century ends become the last queen of the islands. The first chapter moves the action forward thirty years, and we see the newspaper writer's reunion with the queen in Boston. After a year of house arrest in 'Iolani Palace in the wake of the coup by the Missionary Boys, she has come to plead her island nation's case before the outgoing U.S. president.

What transpires in these pages is historical fiction at its finest. The novelist, working at the top of his powers, makes us privy to the private as well as the public side of this story, from the intimacy of this odd pair of old friends—the newsman and the queen—to the fusion of good manners and good politics that comprise the latter's meeting with President Cleveland. Toward the end of these pages that portray with a clear eye such questions as national sovereignty and political justice—questions that still loom large for us today—the book takes a marvelous turn back in time as Julius recollects a musical evening in the royal Hawaiian's Waikiki house, with himself, the queen (a talented composer in her own right), his own cousin, and his cousin's wife singing old songs and new, and raising the level of the narrative to the grand old highway of vital historical fiction.

* * *

As a reader, when you reach the end of a particularly engrossing novel in whose pages you have dwelled for days or weeks, you feel a sense of wholeness and completion, however temporary. Imagine the anguish of a writer who knows, because of illness or other circumstances beyond his control, that he will never complete his latest work in progress. When Isaac Babel, as his biographers describe the harrowing last moments of the great Russian writer's life, was led to a wall deep in the bowels of Moscow's Lyubyanka Prison, he pleaded with his executioners, "Let me finish!"

Ah, yes, yes, whether Stalin or cancer, life has a great variety of monsters that sometimes keep even the best of writers from finishing according to plan. I, for one, am extremely grateful that we have at least these first pages of James Houston's unfinished, and now posthumously published, novel, this beautiful beginning which anneals, as all good art somehow does, the ache of knowing this is all we have of it. Read on, and you will find the same gratitude and pleasure welling up in you, like the night music in the house at Waikiki.

Kapolei, Hawai'i, August 2010

TOUCHING HER: A PROLOGUE

Honolulu Harbor, 1868

I was a young man then, on my first visit to the tropics, and I cannot exaggerate the seductive texture of that night, the water's uncanny stillness, the velvet air upon the skin. Simply standing there put me in a swoon, the moon upon the water, its light spreading out to make a glossy film. A dozen ships floated in that liquid light, each mast tinted by the gloss and the glow, phantom ships, somehow not of this ocean, as if they'd crossed the void between moon and earth, floating downward through the light to find at last a golden anchorage. I know now that the night itself had seduced me long before she emerged from the crowd of dancing couples.

I watched her move across the deck, gliding from partner to partner as if sent forth to make each of them fall for her, one by one. And yet in her effortless and languid turns there was nothing promiscuous. She was not flirting. She gave herself to the dance with a kind of eloquent abandon, her eyes alive with mirth and eagerness and sheer joy in the moment.

Up on the quarter deck a small band of fiddlers and reed men noodled and sawed their way through a medley of tunes I'd heard before, gavottes and jigs and mazurkas and sarabandes, but I'd never seen them danced this way, perfect form without formality, the glowing grace, the bewitching smile. She was a gypsy girl transported from the streets of some Spanish town to the deck of a frigate drawn up to the wharf of this faraway port, in her tight-waisted gown, the neck low cut, the swelling bosom, the jeweled necklace against flawless olive skin, the black and abundant hair gathered high behind her head.

I turned to the fellow who'd brought me along, a cousin from Boston who'd been there in the islands for several years, buying and selling goods from Asia. He knew someone who knew the French captain who'd thrown this moonlit party as a way of welcoming himself and his ship and his crew to Hawai'i. Attorneys were there, and plantation managers, military men with their wives, some public officials, both Hawaiian and white. On this radiant Friday night it was the place to be.

"Do you know that woman," I asked him, "the one dancing with such flair?"

"My wife knows her quite well. That's Lydia Dominis."

"She looks like an islander."

"And indeed she is."

"Well, what sort of name is Dominis? It has a rather Mediterranean ring."

"Italian, I think."

"She's married, then."

"Most definitely."

"And the husband. Is he here? She seems to be dancing with every man on board."

"If the truth be known, they are seldom seen together."

"I wonder why."

"It's a long story."

"Had I a woman who could dance like that I would keep close to her side both day and night."

"Between you and me, the husband is a bit…"

"A bit?"

"Obtuse is perhaps too strong a word."

"Not indifferent, I hope."

"Alas, my dear Julius, indifferent is very close to the mark. And believe me, it has been difficult for her, in a town like this—a village, really—where everyone knows everyone else's business."

As the long medley came to an end, she happened to be standing close by our side of the ship. He grabbed my arm. "Come. Let me introduce you. She's one of the people here you absolutely have to meet."

I held back, suddenly reluctant. "Not now," I murmured, "another time."

"Nonsense," he said, pulling me past two couples. "There's no time like the present."

Her partner had just stepped away for drinks, and before I could protest, the introductions were made. I was a relative newcomer to the islands, a businessman, he explained, as well as a correspondent for one of the Boston papers, which was technically true, though I had yet to file my first report.

Still animated from the dance floor swirl, she said something to the effect that everyone she met these days seemed to be from Boston. Then the lead fiddler was setting a tempo for the next tune, and I saw with a stab of panic that her hands and arms said she was ready. For these few moments she was simply poised between partners, and I was next.

I couldn't move. Dancing with her would be a disaster, the dancing itself. What's more, dancing would mean touching her. I'm ashamed to confess that the thought of this unnerved me, touching skin a few shades darker than my own. Don't ask me why. It was a groundless apprehension, one I can give voice to only now, after all these years, as the memory comes back. I was twenty-seven, and so recently arrived I had yet to touch a woman whose skin was not white.

Could I back away from her? No. It was too late for that. As the music rose again I swallowed my panic, took her hand and placed a hand upon her waist, and in my halting way began to move, thinking that if I made a fool of myself I would be doing so in the arms of the most desired woman at the party.

Luckily for me it was a waltz, one of the few steps I'd actually learned and practiced, though even then with hesitation, thanks to old childhood warnings from my mother and deacon father and all the good, upright members of the home congregation. In their view dancing, like drink and gambling and bodily display and carnal yearning, was yet another temptation placed before us by a treacherous and wily Devil bent on our moral ruin. But something about a foreign port makes it easier to silence such admonitions and set your reserve aside. Something about the balmy air and lagoons and the curve of coco palms says all such diabolical enticements need to be given their fair chance.

With the harbor waters glittering, there was nothing to worry about. My clumsiness didn't matter. Her laughing smile said she forgave me, said, "Have a good time!" It was a form of welcome to this tiny island kingdom.

I was bursting with gratitude, smitten, floating in the same golden light that buoyed up the ships across the water. What could I have been wary of? The color of her skin? As we turned and swayed—ONE two three, ONE two three—her hand against mine was soft and warm. And the touch itself brought me to a place I'd never been, brought me close enough to look into the blackest eyes I'd ever seen. They were large and full of light, emitting the same joyful light that had captivated me. But behind the joy shone something else that hadn't been apparent from afar. As we moved across the deck, I saw that her irises, darker than ebony, were also lit with a black fire. I know now, thirty years later, that these are eyes you can easily fall for, as did every man on board that night. But you fall in love with them at your peril.

I would watch this same fire fuel her undoing. It came from another place, another time, from a world much older than the one we all inhabit now, from a time when an ancient ocean culture was still intact. Though educated in a missionary school, she was descended from a long line of chiefs, a woman of Polynesia who from early in life had learned the ways of the West. She could read Shakespeare and Jane Austen, but she had not forgotten her family's genealogy. She could sit barefooted on a woven mat, dip her fingers into a calabash of thick poi, lift out a gob and suck her fingers clean. And she could sit at an ambassador's table and know which fork to use for salad, which knife for fish. Though no one could have foreseen it on the night we met, she would rise to become Hawaii's last queen. She would take the name Lili'uokalani, which means "eyes burned by heaven." In that role her shows of fiery and fierce determination would become intolerable to the diplomats and lawyers and Honolulu merchants who took it upon themselves to bring her down. (Some would be the sons of men mingling with us on the frigate's deck that very night!) That simmering fire bespoke a warrior spirit they knew they would never be able to manage or manipulate so long as she was on the throne.

PART ONE

AT THE PARK SQUARE STATION

Boston, 1896

With one exception, it has been my habit for many years to destroy all letters, both personal and business, as soon as they are answered. It is a strange practice, I know, and friends have often chided me. Why bother sharing anything of consequence, they complain, if you'll be setting a match to it within the week? I'm not sure why I burn them. Maybe it's my futile effort to manage the unmanageable clutter here. Maybe I am wary of their sentiments. Maybe I need to surround myself with rings of flaming pages.

The only exception has been my correspondence with Lydia Dominis, who, after all too brief a reign, is known by that name once again, though I still think of her, and refer to her, as do so many thousands of Hawaiians in her homeland, as the Queen. Destroying her messages would be unthinkable. They have nourished me in ways I can't explain. They are stored here in the deep side drawer, quite a stack of them now, each one beginning "My Dear Julius," some on her private scented stock, some on Palace stationery with its royal crest, the paper heavy and embossed, her script embellished with loops and flourishes. Among the more recent is a Western Union telegram delivered toward the end of 1896 with word that she would be arriving Christmas Day, on the evening train from New York, and would I be able to meet her at the Park Square Station.

I confess that this flustered me, catching me entirely off guard. I was flattered too. My tears welled up. I hadn't heard from her in months, hadn't seen her in nearly two years, and then only at a distance, her captors keeping the world at bay.

I of course wired back that I would be there, though I had to wonder why she'd chosen this season of the year to visit New England. To be sure, there is the family tie. She has Boston relatives of whom she's very fond. When they received word from the West Coast, early in December, that she'd once again set foot on American soil, they immediately invited her to spend the holidays, half expecting, I think, that she would decline, with an entire continent still to be crossed. But she didn't decline. You might say the railways made it easy for her, vying to be her carrier, offering luxury accommodations in the hope that other travelers would be induced to ride the same train an ex-queen once rode. In the end she chose Sunset Limited, taking the southern route by way of New Orleans and Atlanta, and now was bound for Boston in the first week of winter. There was more to this than a family visit, I told myself. There had to be.

It was snowing when her telegram arrived, the bundled messenger boy blue in the face, shivering as if he might collapse at my feet. It was still snowing when I reached the station, icy flakes blown sideways in a biting wind off the harbor. I could not help but remember the one Christmas I'd spent in Honolulu, celebrated under skies of purest blue, with cottony clouds gathered above the inland peaks, the season's colors provided by oblong leaves of vivid green framing red bursts of the hibiscus flower.

Behind the screech and hissing clang of the engine three passenger cars slowed with a lurch and settled, a short train, on a night when most people had by that time tucked away the turkey dinner and were staying put, safe and snug by the parlor fire.

As luck would have it, I found myself standing close by the steam-clouded window of her compartment. She seemed to be peering out, searching the platform. With the glass so blurred, it was hard to tell. I raised my hand, and she raised hers, as if in greeting, though perhaps to adjust her hat. She loves hats, carries them for all occasions: sun hats, walking hats, feathery hats with elaborate plumage. It occurred to me that if this were an extended trip she would be traveling with boxes of hats. And I was right. Before long, enough luggage was stacked upon the platform for a trip around the world. But in advance of that a Negro porter had let down the short stairway at the end of the car, then stepped out to hold the door for a brown-skinned man of a somewhat lighter hue, a slender Hawaiian in a long traveling coat and woolen scarf, sporting a thick handlebar moustache.

I recognized him—Joseph something (a multisyllabled Hawaiian name with more vowels than consonants). We had met once or twice in Honolulu when the *Transcript* sent me out there to cover the overthrow, hopefully to shed some light for Boston readers on the ensuing turmoil in that faraway archipelago. He was the Queen's personal manager and financial agent both before and after she was forced to abdicate.

Now her foot was on the stair, and I would have made a move to help her down, but this was clearly Joseph's domain. Her eyes were on her boots as her gloved hand clutched his. When she was very young she'd fallen from a swing. Her left leg had been injured and never properly healed, and in later life she began to favor it, at moments like this, or when fatigue got the best of her.

She wore a woolen cloak with a broad fur collar and a round winter hat somewhat in the Russian style, which sat high to contain the hair piled beneath. Though she usually wears it coiled, her hair, when loose, is still long and thick and black, laced here and there with threads of white. Her mouth is still full in the Polynesian way, with a characteristic lift along the upper lip. Her skin is still remarkably smooth, free of blemishes, the olive-tinted skin of a younger woman. The burden of her years shows in the lidded angle of her eyes. I will say this right now: she carries in her face and in her eyes and in her voice a grief for all that has befallen her people during the past century and more. There is a weight upon her soul that is never lifted. And yet this is not the kind of grief that forces itself upon you, coupled as it is with a radiance that can emerge at any time, telling you she has not been defeated by this history. Her liquid eyes are still capable of immense pleasure, and now they glittered with moisture, as did my own. Her smile was wide and gracious, as if she'd been saving it all for me.

Among Hawaiians an intimacy of feeling is always close to the surface, ready to spill forth, and they do not conceal it. This quality of spirit is both their beauty and their undoing, this readiness to give more of themselves than has been asked for. In our Western world, alas, there have been too many who see such soft-heartedness as a shortcoming, a trait to be exploited. I hope I am no longer among them. I hope my time spent in the Pacific taught me how to receive such generosity. It is what they look for at any moment of meeting, the readiness to be with them in that same openhearted place they call Aloha.

That was her first word to me as we met upon the platform under the vaulted ceiling of the Park Square Station. "Aloha," her voice as captivating as her glance, a musical voice. "Aloha, Julius. How good of you to come and meet us here on such a horrid night."

Scarcely had I time to say "Aloha, Your Majesty" before her hands were on my shoulders, drawing me toward her, so that our foreheads touched and our noses pressed nostril to nostril.

She held me there, and I held her until she stepped back and said, "You remember Joseph."

"Indeed, I do. Aloha, and welcome to Boston."

Taking his cue from the Queen he now approached with the same gentle word of greeting and pressed his forehead and nose to mine, as did the third member of their party, who had just then joined us, a handsome Hawaiian woman of fifty years or so who was the Queen's attendant.

I felt blessed to be in their company, so quickly admitted to this little circle of warmth somehow transported from the tropics to our northern clime. At the same time, I was glancing up and down the platform, relieved to see so few witnesses to this display which certain of my colleagues might consider barbaric. Kinkaid in particular came to mind, the sardonic and red-cheeked columnist whose comment might well have been, "A man's nostril is nobody's business but his own."

I had a carriage waiting. As it turned out, we needed two. Joseph rode with the luggage. I rode with the Queen and her companion (whom I shall call Mrs. K). We talked first about the snow, how long it had been falling, how long it might continue, how it slowed our cross-town journey, and how Mrs. K had never before been so close to snow, having seen it only once, on a trip to Hawai'i, the southernmost island in the chain, at a time when the two volcanic peaks of Mauna Loa and Mauna Kea happened to be capped with white.

Snow was the last thing I cared to talk about, but with Mrs. K so close beside us in the carriage, it wasn't a time to voice the hundred questions in my mind. As a journalist of sorts I am by nature a nosey person, a rabid consumer of details large and small. I'd last seen her when I'd returned to Honolulu to cover the trial. Whether or not she'd seen me there, I still wasn't sure. I still longed to know what had happened during the months of her confinement, whatever she might be willing to reveal. I knew she'd been held incommunicado for almost a year, few visitors, no papers, no mail. I also knew she didn't like to be interrogated, believing all things that need to be said will sooner or later find their way into the random flow of conversation.

So we nattered on about this and that, the small courtesies, inquiries about mutual acquaintances, how long she'd be staying, and I had the chance to observe her at rather close range, struck by how she held herself against the leather backrest, at ease, yet not entirely relaxed, with a sense of contained expectancy, her hands in her lap as if holding some small package, delicate and fragile, that soon would have to be delivered.

A QUEEN IS ALWAYS NEWS

The Parker House is our best hotel. For years our most eminent writers lunched there once a week, Longfellow among them, Holmes and Emerson, James Russell Lowell. Merely to be seated within view of their table was a badge of honor, and the aura, the cultivated glamour of those days still lingers. The hotel's guest list includes numerous dignitaries from Paris, from Rome, London and Madrid. Yet royal visitors have been extremely rare. On this night the manager himself had interrupted his holiday in order to be standing at the counter, to welcome her, to check her in, to supervise the transport of luggage from the carriageway to an upper floor. Across the lobby half a dozen rumpled reporters had risen from their lounge chairs and sofas as if roused from a long slumber. Ordinarily I would have been among them, and I knew they wondered how I had penetrated the entourage, standing close beside her as she signed in.

With a weary smile she murmured, "All across the country they have followed me like hunting dogs."

"They have no shame," I said, "hanging about like this on Christmas night. Shall I tell them to be gone? It's almost ten."

She looked at me as if hoping I'd do just that, but then said, "No. No, perhaps this is as good a time as any. Tell them to pass along their cards. I'll need twenty minutes or so."

It was her second visit to Boston. She remembered the Parker House and had reserved a corner suite which, if the weather ever lifted, would offer a fine view toward the harbor. ("I like to see water moving," she once told me. "The land stays still, and the water moves. It is the two together that tells the story of where you are.")

A fire was crackling in the grate, the mantel above it framed with wide-mouthed lilies. There was holly on the sideboard, sprigs of mistletoe tied to the chandelier, and a huge bouquet of red and white carnations filling the room with a heady scent. Where they'd come from I couldn't say—with a blizzard now howling past the window they seemed miraculous to me—but I recognized the handiwork of the small, beaming woman who stood beside the table, holding forth a garland of carnations woven to make a Hawaiian lei, which she placed around the Queen's neck, kissing her on both cheeks. Sarah Lee had never been to Hawai'i—indeed, she'd never been west of Buffalo—but she knew how to welcome a visitor from the middle of the Pacific.

Her husband stood behind her, rather more stiffly, I would say, not quite sure what his role should be, a lanky fellow who leaned over his wife as if the forward angle of his body were in itself sufficient greeting. William is in his seventies, a partner in one of our more distinguished publishing firms, and cousin to the Queen's late husband, whose family came from Massachusetts, as have so many of the families who now control the terrain—some would say the future—of the Hawaiian Islands. (I will have to come back to this, to the strangeness of their family tie, the unlikely kinship of a Polynesian queen and a Boston publisher, since it bears not only on the pattern of her life but on a strange and fateful bond that has linked Hawaiʻi and New England for a century and more.)

After the handshakes and hugs and introductions and exclamations of greeting—"Merry Christmas!" "Mele kalikimaka!"—after the luggage had been disposed of and the porter tipped, we all headed for a meeting room where the reporters had been told to wait. The Queen leaned heavily on Sarah's arm, the day of travel catching up with her, and Sarah urged her toward a plush divan, soft and cozy. But the Queen chose position over comfort, an upright chair with upholstered backing and seat and armrests, a throne-like chair that elevated her above the press corps, who sat opposite, pencils and notebooks at the ready.

Sarah Lee spoke first, standing beside the chair like a chamberlain, straight as a tree, gull-gray hair pulled back, hands clasped below her bosom. She was ignited by this reunion, her eyes warm with affection for the one she hadn't seen in ten years, her voice animated, a seasoned voice.

"It's a grand day for Boston, and a grand day for our family, to have our dear, dear cousin beside us once again. We had not imagined she would be meeting with you all so soon. But she has graciously agreed and she welcomes any comments or questions you may have."

From the way the Queen regarded them you would never know this was her first encounter with newsmen since the trial. She hadn't spoken with a reporter in two or three years. In San Francisco, where she'd stopped for ten days, she had granted no interviews. On the cross-country train, journalists had dogged her all the way, eager to know what had brought her to the United States, sometimes standing on the platform waiting for the Sunset Limited, sometimes boarding the train, hoping to catch her unawares in the dining car. A traveling queen was news, even an ex-queen. We Americans, so proud of having fled Europe to leave behind all vestiges of pomp and courtly excess, with our alleged disdain for the display and privilege of kings and queens and dukes and duchesses, we will nonetheless gather around like moths to the lamplight to behold even the afterglow of royalty.

Though she had so far spoken with no one, stories had appeared. Excerpts from so-called personal interviews had been quoted, and those quotes reprinted. I think that's why, in spite of the hour and the long day's journey, she had agreed to sit a while and talk, as a way to clear the air, put to rest the rumors, weary of untruths and half-truths composed in haste by writers with deadlines and determined to file *some*thing.

She wore a black tailored skirt and jacket, accented by Sarah's carnation lei and a smaller lei made of tiny feathers tightly woven, red, green, and gold, which seemed to intrigue an editor from *The Globe*. He wondered if it had some special significance.

Her hand reached up to stroke it and she said yes, on

a trip such as this she wears it every day, her one mark of royalty.

"It takes years to make one of these, you know. The feathers are only found in one place, under the wings of nectar-sucking forest birds. And then but one is found under each of the wings from which they are plucked. So they are rare and very precious. You might call it our jewelry. These same feathers are used to line the gold and crimson royal cloak that has been passed down from ruler to ruler for many generations."

The *Globe* editor had seen this as a simple question, light and personal, to break the ice. I think he half expected it might require some translation. He'd been in town long enough to remember an earlier visit, back in 1887, when King David Kalakaua still ruled the islands. The king's wife, Kapiʻolani, had been invited to London to join the world's royalty at Queen Victoria's Jubilee celebration. En route she'd stopped in Boston. It was Kapiʻolani's first and only trip abroad, and all along the way she too had been courted by the press. But alas, she spoke no English, or rather she chose not to. A proud and elegant woman, also descended from a long line of chiefs, she took it as a point of honor, one way of keeping her distance from the encroaching ways of the West. For the American reporters who flocked to interview her, the strange music of the Hawaiian tongue coupled with her dusky features made Kapiʻolani more a novelty than a source of useful information. I know that's what the *Globe* editor was remembering. He had forgotten that most of the translating had been handled by her traveling companion and sister to the king, Liliʻuokalani, in those days still a princess.

He was seeing her now as if for the first time, and her reply had impressed him, as had the dignity she summoned as she spoke. Her body seemed to rise past its own fatigue. She has an extraordinary bearing and air of command, and the very fact that she could utter well-formed English sentences took them all by surprise. I could see it on their faces. I know these fellows. They think Boston is the center of the universe and bring knowing eyes and a bit of a smirk to a meeting with the deposed ruler of a tiny kingdom some six thousand miles away, still sometimes referred to as "The Cannibal Islands."

A flurry of questions now followed: Why was she in Boston? How long did she plan to stay? Did she have other travel plans? Would she perhaps be stopping in Washington, D.C., as had been widely reported?

At the moment, she told them, her plans were open-ended. The capital was a possibility. But nothing was fixed. She certainly had no appointments there.

"And yet," said the *Globe* editor, "you wear the royal feather lei. In some sense aren't you traveling as one who is still the queen, or sees herself as queen? In some unofficial way, might you still be representing your people?"

With an enormous smile she said she wanted one thing made perfectly clear: her trip had no political significance. She was there in Boston solely at the invitation of her dear cousins, and the timing was ideal, since she'd always wanted to visit the Northeast during winter. She was there to spend a while with relatives and to rest. As for how long, she wasn't sure. Into January. Perhaps longer. Her plans were fluid. As for the rumor that she might travel on to England to visit Princess Kaiʻulani, currently completing her studies there, well, this was still possible—"She is my only niece, and I have missed her"—but reports that she'd already booked passage were, like so many others they may have heard, simply untrue.

Her black eyes held them, as did her captivating voice, which can take on the low rhythm of a chant. She never raises it. To emphasize a point she will use silence, a bit of space between one phrase and the next, compelling you to listen. When she stopped talking they all waited a while, expecting the next sentence. Finally another fellow broke the spell.

Could she comment at all, he asked, on the political and economic situation in Hawai'i, now that it is a republic rather than a monarchy? "We understand that the new government does not have a great deal of popular support."

For these past three years, she said, she'd been what you might call in retirement and so far removed from public life she'd had no chance to form an opinion one way or the other. Even if she did possess current facts about political matters in her homeland her view would be of little importance, since she was now traveling as a private citizen. She'd decided to make no comment.

At the phrase "in retirement" I could see pencils pause above the notebook pages, see eyebrows lifting and the exchange of cynical glances. Though she sounded sincere, she seemed to be contradicting all we knew of her. This was the woman whose monarchy had been overthrown by a coalition of island businessmen in collusion with the United States Marines, the woman who'd been arrested for supporting acts of rebellion against the very men who had deposed her. To say that her views no longer mattered, to claim that she'd withdrawn from the fray, was hard for me to swallow.

To be truthful, I didn't believe her at all, nor did any of my colleagues, who now began to press a bit harder than they may at first have intended.

"According to one report from the *San Francisco Examiner,* you are in fact on your way to Washington, D.C., to claim for yourself a kind of pension..." (this was Bobby Kinkaid, the *Herald's* red-cheeked columnist) "...a sort of compensation from the United States for its role in...how should we say... your royal loss?"

She touched her feather lei again and for the first time dropped her eyes. "Yes, I have read that report. It is from an interview compiled by a writer I have never spoken with and never met, a product, I suppose, of his own imagination."

Kinkaid, known for his bulldog persistence, tried again. "Let me put it another way, Your Majesty. We all know there are men in Washington quite eager to annex the Hawaiian Islands. If that happens, would it not extinguish the last hope that your monarchy might be restored...in which case the federal government would be obliged to make some sort of recompense..."

Here she raised her hand, as if gathering her thoughts. But the words that came next were unintelligible to Kinkaid and his fellows. As if she'd lost her grasp of English, she was speaking in Hawaiian. She glanced at Sarah and then at me, a desperate glance.

Another reporter chimed in, "Your Majesty, perhaps you could simply give us your views on annexation itself, not a political analysis but, rather, your personal perspective. We have heard that there are many in your homeland who oppose it...Hawaiians who still claim loyalty to you."

This time her answer was inaudible. Her voice wavered,

and into her eyes came a look I thought I recognized, having seen others released from prolonged confinement, as if the gaze of these reporters became too much for her, the prying eyes and prying minds of men she didn't know and couldn't trust. It was a hunted look, a prisoner's wariness of the outside world, wondering who is the ally, who the adversary, fearful that anyone in the room might turn on her at any moment and she could be accused again, convicted again, put away again.

I looked at Sarah, expecting her to intervene, but she couldn't move, her eyes too had filled with fear of she knew not what. I stood up and told them Her Majesty had reached the end of a long day and was grateful for their interest in her visit. "Perhaps there will be other opportunities to speak with her. But this interview has come to a close. If you have further questions you all know how to reach me."

And indeed they did. Ordinarily I would now join two or three of them for a quick one at the hotel bar before heading out into the weather. In their jaded eyes I could see the question: How has Julius so suddenly become the royal spokesman? But they held their tongues and folded shut their notebooks. For this night they'd had enough.

The Queen, still seated, and much relieved, had no desire to move just yet. When she took my hand her palm was wet. "Thank you so much."

"I didn't mean to say all that."

"I'm glad you did."

This was a murmur, meant for my ears alone, as if some long-held secret agreement had now been fulfilled.

"I hope you're joining us for dinner."

"I think not. The family needs to have you to themselves."

"Tomorrow, then. You must come for tea."

"It would be my honor."

She stood, leaning on Sarah's arm, favoring her leg, with a last gracious wave to the press corps, who'd been waiting for her exit.

Kinkaid sidled up to me then, his cheeks aglow, a hint of mischief in his thin smile.

"What is this, Julius?"

"What is what?"

"You here doing a story?"

"I'm always doing a story."

"For just a moment there you were making the officious noises of a press secretary."

"It was time to wind it up, don't you think? They have a late supper waiting in the dining room."

"But something rattled her. This annexation business. Why couldn't she talk about it, at least throw us a bone to gnaw on? Everyone knows the boys in D.C. are champing at the bit to get their hands on Hawai'i and get a permanent base for our ships out there before the Japs do."

I wanted to say she'll say whatever she has to say when she's ready to say it. Instead I said, "I'll suggest that she issue a statement sometime soon, just to set the record straight."

"There you go again."

"Again?"

"Sounding like her press secretary."

"Well, Bobby Boy, with fellows like you on her tail, maybe she's going to need one."

MY SPEAR OF WORDS

Kinkaid was right. He saw where I was headed before I saw it myself. Once those first reports hit the stands, calls and queries came in from every quarter, from magazines and socialites, from church leaders and politicians inviting her to a reception here, a concert there, "a small dinner party to meet some of our most prominent citizens." She hadn't foreseen this, had no staff to handle it. Joseph, her business manager and financial agent, was overwhelmed, a charming fellow, quick-witted and good with numbers, but new to this country, new to the tenacity of American journalists. He knew nothing at all about Boston and who was who, who had to be pampered, who could be ignored.

By the next afternoon it had already started, giving us only the briefest time to begin our catching up, just the two of us, sipping tea, as we'd so often done in the islands, though now brittle snowflakes swirled against the hotel window. She was leaning to pour, glancing at me through the curl of steam.

"I hope you can forgive me, Julius."

"There's nothing to forgive. You're here, and it's wonderful to see you again."

She shook her head. "I should have alerted you much sooner about the train. And then…of all days to invade your life."

"My best Christmas present in years, believe me!"

"Once I knew they were going to let me travel…the last days there…I left in such a rush with no time for anything. In truth I have been meaning to write for months now and thank you for the essays."

"Ah yes, my long-lost essays. I wasn't sure they'd reached you. But then Joseph sent a very cordial note."

"It was all I dared to send. They are quite inflammatory, you know—your writings—in certain circles there."

"I would hope so."

"My mail was being tampered with, my every move spied upon. It was a miracle your packet arrived somehow intact, and I of course read them eagerly, more than once. Then came the trial and for almost a year it was impossible to send a message of any kind."

Her eyelids closed, as in prayer, as if to pray away old demons, and then sprang open. "But I had your words hidden among my belongings, and they gave me hope, simply knowing someone from afar had seen what was going on. You know what is said about me in the Honolulu papers, and in the San Francisco papers, where they merely repeat what the Missionary Boys tell them. Your voice is not at all like theirs."

And here she began to quote a passage, one she'd

memorized word for word from one of my own dispatches to the *Transcript,* her voice slowing as she spoke, making it a kind of incantation:

"'The American people are deceived, blindly and falsely advised by every mail which leaves these islands. Is it to be expected that revolutionists who will seize the reins of government, turn Gatling guns against a constitutional monarchy, and confiscate all copies of the *New York Herald* will stop at such a trifle as the inspection of all press dispatches?'"

Her near-singing of these sentences written two years back caused my arm hairs to prickle and my scalp to tingle, and again she was leaning toward me, her eyes searching mine as she held the teapot, ready to refill our cups, this time so near, her scent—something floral, gardenia, or plumeria—blended with the pekoe-scented steam. She was close enough to kiss when there came an ill-timed knocking at the door, and I cursed whoever it might be.

Before we could stop her, Mrs. K had emerged from her room to admit an obsequious bellman who held upon his palm a silver platter and on the platter a display of small envelopes. Soon they were spread across the table between us, a dozen notes from other guests, on engraved Parker House stationery, wondering when might be a convenient time to call. As if suddenly exhausted she fell back against the couch, amused by these attentions but aggravated too, flinging a hand to brush them all away.

"What can I do, Julius? I don't have the energy for this."

"Perhaps a select few could be invited..."

"No. Not now. Not yet."

"It might avoid being accosted in the dining room."

"I won't use the dining room. I'll take dinner here."

"Why don't you let me handle this?"

"Could you? Would you? You must have a thousand things to do."

"It won't take any time at all."

In fact, it took about an hour. To make each reply sound official I signed my name at the bottom, above an invented title which turned out to be prophetic: "Her Majesty's Secretary."

After that, one thing led quickly to the next. She needed a less-exposed location, away from the center of town, and the Lees wanted her closer to their Beacon Street address out in Brookline. They knew of a cottage, a cozy place on a tree-lined street, with a pitched roof, white clapboard siding, a front yard bordered by a picket fence. The next day she made the move, though how long she'd stay was anyone's guess. She was renting by the week while her mail continued to arrive at the Parker House, an abundance of mail, which was fine with the manager, who figured serving as the royal address had to be good for business.

It fell to me to pick up the daily bundle and hand-carry it to her cottage, a twenty-minute trolley ride out along Beacon Street and twenty minutes to return, sometimes longer, depending on the weather and the state of the snow. My first thought was I didn't have time for such an errand, such a simple task, fit for any kind of hireling. Yet it bespoke a remarkable trust, given all she'd been through. Not only had her mail been screened and censored, her life had several times been threatened. After the arrest, her house had been ransacked, her papers seized. It struck me then that a Hansel and

Gretel cottage on the outskirts of Boston was exactly what she needed, with some time to hibernate far from the prying eyes of Honolulu, where they'd tried, and failed, to break her.

To be entrusted with her mail was no small honor. "And who else can I call on?" she asked, with pleading eyes.

So of course I made adjustments. When you are your own taskmaster you often put in longer hours than the man who works from eight to five. But you can arrange those hours any way you like. In the years since my wife passed away I've lived alone in this small apartment behind the Custom House, freelancing, as they say, patching this and that together. I take assignments when they come along. As a sometime "Contributor" and "Special Correspondent" to the *Transcript* I do most of my work here, as well as manage a few family properties that have come down to me. On my stationery the word "Offices" refers to these three disheveled rooms I occupy with my typewriter, my filing drawers, my shelves of books, my view across India Street toward the thirty-one pillars of the Custom House with its arching dome.

* * *

In short, I found the time to make this daily visit, and soon other duties followed, as I served by turn as mailman, as secretary, as press agent, sometimes as semi-official companion, sitting beside her bundled up for a sledding party, or her escort for an evening at the theater. She so often called upon me I couldn't help but ask, in my heart of hearts, was I not at least some small part of the reason she'd come this far? I wasn't sure. Perhaps I didn't dare be sure. She is still a queen, I would tell myself, with a queenly manner that must sometimes be asserted, obliging all of us to wait upon her. I was not a citizen of Hawai'i, not among those—like Joseph and Mrs. K—who might once have been her "royal subjects." Yet I carried a deep allegiance to that distant place, to *her* place, and thus to her (and which came first I cannot say, even now, after all this time has passed). I'd been down to Washington to cover the debate about Hawaii's future. I'd been writing pamphlets and broadsides and letters to the *New York Times,* as well as to our congressmen—my own self-assumed crusade. And the Queen, for months and months, had been often on my mind. Though she'd reentered my life when I least expected it, I'm now inclined to view it as foreordained, as if by sheer powers of concentration and recollection I'd drawn her, magnetized her toward me from the far Pacific.

I should make it clear that my recent stays in Honolulu—to cover the overthrow, then to cover her trial for treason—had started me tinkering with a second book. The first hadn't been a real book, after all, a mere gathering of those dispatches from 1894 and '95, composed on the run. This time I imagined a full-length study of modern-day Hawai'i and how its fate bears upon our national agenda, this mad dream of an American empire that reaches so far beyond our natural borders and halfway across to Asia. The Queen was central, a woman of Polynesia whose tiny realm is under siege, trying to preserve the monarchy and save her people in the face of overwhelming odds. Teddy Roosevelt would be in it and Henry Cabot Lodge and Grover Cleveland and the men he scolded so severely for their outlaw maneuver. It would draw on what I knew of her as well as what I knew of them—she called them the Missionary Boys—their divided hearts and their calculating minds. I believed I knew them well enough since I could have been one myself.

My father could have been among the fathers and grandfathers of those who now claim Hawai'i as their own. He was an upright and devoutly Christian man—God rest his soul!—an unsparing moralist who also had a taste for travel. He could easily have boarded a brig out of Boston Harbor and sailed with them around Cape Horn, taken up residence in Kailua or Lahaina, and I could have been born there and raised a missionary's son. I came that close.

Those men who brought the Gospel to the mid-Pacific, they all came from our New England towns, from congregations of worshippers who still sit in the same pews I sat in for so many years. Their hymns were my hymns—"Amazing Grace," "Blest Be the Tie That Binds"—songs that still stir the blood, stir up old longings when I hear them or find myself singing the lyrics as I walk along an empty street, the music of my boyhood days.

In this imagined book of mine I had no desire to fault those pioneering fathers. I've met numerous men from that generation. When I was five I met Hiram Bingham, who first translated the Bible into Hawaiian and had returned to Boston after twenty years out there. He was not a cynic or a hypocrite. A strict but passionate man, he loved words and he loved to sing. In our parlor, to entertain my sister and me, he once sang some hymns he'd translated, and oh, how we laughed at the marvelously barbaric syllables coming from his ministerial mouth. Men of his time, in their obsessive need to recreate native people in their own image, were of course misguided, perhaps deranged. But they were not deceitful, as their sons and grandsons have become, the descendants born in Hawai'i, who grew up there, acquired great parcels of land, and now see themselves as the rightful and exclusive heirs to all of it, every field and plain and peak and valley and sandy beach. They will come back here for their schooling, at Yale or Harvard or Williams or Amherst, then return to those emerald islands in the farthest sea like princes returning to their rightful domain.

That much I still have in common with the missionary sons: I too have been eager to return. Before she arrived I'd been scheming for yet another assignment from the *Transcript*, foreseeing long meetings with her and with the men behind the move to annexation. I saw myself bareheaded at the rail as the ship glides again into Honolulu Harbor, a crusader ready to plunge my spear of words into the hearts of those who'd replaced her government with one of their own...

Then came the telegram, and suddenly she was here, in Massachusetts, on my side of North America, changing all my plans, my schemes, my dreams.

WAITING FOR SIGNS

Before long I'd dropped almost everything else that once had seemed so urgent, spending more hours in Brookline than I spent in town. Each day began at the round walnut table, as I helped her sort through it all, considering which interviews to grant, which visitors to receive, if any, answering more than half these inquiries in my own hand. In this way we could pass an entire morning, Mrs. K would set out cups of tea, and if you had glanced through the latticed window we might have appeared to be husband and wife sorting through the season's greeting cards.

They came from reporters, relentlessly seeking access, and by the dozens from Boston women eager to socialize. After the first local stories had been picked up by papers in other cities, letters began to arrive from all across the land, from autograph hunters and photograph hunters, invitations of every type, harangues, critiques, salutes and prayers, offers of money and requests for money. Some supported her right to rule, while others condemned her treasonous and primitive ways:

> I am sick and tired of hearing about "The Hawaiian problem" (wrote one fellow from San Francisco). If you think this trip will get you any sympathy from the American people, you are wasting your time. You brought it all upon yourself!

"What did I tell you," she said to me. "He has been reading the *Examiner*."

Seated on either side of the daily pile we would pen our polite or not-so-polite replies, make jokes from time to time, share loose thoughts or bits of memory called forth by a name or by a small detail, our random dialogue a curious kind of daily dance, both of us waiting for signs. She seemed to be in limbo, with no clear course ahead, yet from the way she watched the mail I could see that being holed up there was more than a wintertime lying low and licking of wounds. As the days went by, I listened and probed as discreetly as I could, hoping to tease from her some further hint of what was truly on her mind, how long she planned to stay, whether she'd come east to fend off annexation or save her throne or secure for herself some sort of throneless pension or perhaps to travel on to England to conspire with Princess Kaiʻulani, her niece and heir-apparent. Or all of these. Or none of these.

For reading she wore gold-rimmed spectacles which flattered her looks in a scholarly way. One morning she raised her eyes from the page before her, pushed these spectacles onto her forehead, up against the glossy edge of black hair streaked with silver, turned toward the window with a gaze of scholarly distraction, and said something about the weather, the heavy cloud cover that had gathered overnight. After a moment, as if an afterthought, glancing at me, glancing away, she said, "Have I mentioned that I did some writing?"

"Not to my recollection, no. What sort of writing?"

"During my confinement…a number of songs. It's a great comfort, writing songs. And then, I don't know why, I began a kind of story. I have been meaning to tell you… though it's hard to describe…in that room on the upper floor of the palace my brother built. Before they painted over my windowpanes, it was full of light…"

Here her voice fell off. Her brow furrowed.

"And is this the story you began to write? The days of your imprisonment?"

"Much more than that, Julius, much more."

Outside a wind was rising, swelling toward a storm. Loud gusts hurled snow against the window, so that I had to pull my chair around the table, up close to hers, to hear the words, now so soft and slow.

"They painted my windows to prevent me from seeing out. But maybe it helped me to see something else. I have pages and pages that I have carried with me…I think it will be the story of my whole life."

"How far do you mean to go—when you say your whole life?"

I was almost shouting, as the wind howled louder, yet her voice went softer still, both reluctant and eager. "It isn't as easy as one might think, to tell the story of your life, not like writing a song, which sometimes can come into your mind all at once, the music and the roll of the words one and the same, a gift from heaven. The unfolding of your life, all the people in it, you have these memories that seem so clear until you start looking for the best way. It takes time and a place to sit. That is the only thing about these months I am thankful for..."

"When you say the best way?"

"To set the record straight."

The black fire came into her eyes as she began to spill forth a head full and a heart full of places and opinions, a picture of a story that veered in so close to what I myself had been envisioning that it caused my neck hairs to rise again. Had we, in our separate minds, been seeing the same book? From the same world? With the same cast of characters, the century of Hawaiian kings and queens, the politicians and Missionary Boys? It seemed uncanny, that we could be joined in this mutual vision, and yet my heart sank, hearing my own project sink beneath the waves of her quietly fierce and confessional eagerness. Perhaps I could put mine aside, I thought, at least for a while. Or perhaps not. Perhaps just let it go. Could I do that? Let it go? This story, however it might be told, was clearly hers, not mine. And yet had I not brought my own fervor to the task, and thereby earned a kind of claim?

When I didn't speak she said, "Come now, Julius. Please tell me what you think. Honestly. Is it something I should continue with?"

"No question about it. And if I can be of any assistance, if I can be helpful in any way...that is, if you are willing..."

"In due time, yes. Perhaps. What would I do without you?

Just to know you're here. But what I have so far are only notes, only notes. After my release I had to put it all aside, my rooms at home in such a turmoil, all my papers gone or strewn about. They had come through like looters in the night. Only now can I get back to it. The trip across the country showed me something. Have you ever crossed America by train?"

"Indeed I have..."

"Of course, forgive me. You came to visit us..."

"Across and back again, four or five times, in fact, and every time I'm more amazed by the size and range of it all."

"Yes, exactly! You know what I mean! So much land! So much abundance! We have a letter here from a man in Los Angeles. I was there last month, looking out the window. And do you know what I saw?"

"I remember orange trees."

"Yes, groves and groves of them, orange trees without end. In New Mexico I saw the ranchlands where cattle graze by the thousands. I watched it all go by, Texas and Louisiana and Alabama and the Carolinas. And I began to think that I might address my story to this great and powerful nation, with all its rich and fertile land, so much of it still empty, waiting to be occupied. Perhaps I could ask these men in Washington why they want to possess our tiny string of islands which would barely fill the state of Massachusetts. You know what I mean! I know you do!"

Indeed I did. This passionate question, embedded in the story she hoped to tell, was embedded in mine too, that is, in the book I would have started that winter had she not come along. We both knew the answer. Kinkaid had put his finger on it: a permanent base out there in the middle of the ocean. For decades they'd had their eyes on one nearly landlocked and marvelously protected lagoon some called the Pearl River Basin, some called Pearl Harbor, envisioned as the ideal fueling station and naval anchorage. I'd seen it on my first visit to the islands. We'd seen it together, picnicked there under palms and watched a lone fisherman in his outrigger canoe far across the water, his paddle dipping, dipping, dipping into the placid sheen.

HAWAIIAN CODE

Two days later she handed me a sheaf of pages. "Not all of what I have, you understand, so much of it is still just notes and scribbles unintelligible to anyone but me."

That same night, back in my apartment, I read them through, brought to tears by the touching quality of her voice and the very nature of what she'd set out to do. I'd read her long plea to Grover Cleveland, and her speech to the trial board refuting the charges brought against her—both well-crafted, politically astute, by a woman who knew her mind and knew her history. But this was different, more intimate, starting with her mother and father, the brothers and sisters and the Chiefs' Children's School set up by missionary teachers, where they were all sent to study and where she surely first read books like the one she now aspired to write. Call it an autobiography. Her people are skilled tellers of oral tales and keepers of genealogies, but to my knowledge no one of her ancestry had ever tried to set down in full detail the story of one's life. It is an alien idea, imported from afar, yet the spirit of her writing, from the outset, was Hawaiian, already felt in those earliest notes, which began like this:

> The extinct crater or mountain which forms the background to the city of Honolulu is known as The Punchbowl. Very near to its site, on September 2, 1838, I was born.

Notice how she locates herself, by naming the nearest crater. Before her parents are named, there is a nod to volcanic origins.

I was up all night reading and rereading. An hour before dawn a great relief poured through me. I simply let go of any hold I thought I might have and said yes to myself—yes, this was how her story should be told and thus the story of her island home, not by me or by any other foreign writer, observing from near or far, but by the Queen in her own voice. The saga of modern Hawai'i was not mine to tell but hers. She had lived it. What mattered most was that it all come out and find its way into the world. I knew such a story would have enormous appeal for William Lee, her cousin by marriage. He'd brought out my Hawaiian essays (still in print, by the way, and selling well), and his wife Sarah had done the editing. I would mention it to them straightaway, foreseeing a kind of team effort that could move this book along its path. And what better place for her to sit still and get some writing done than a Brookline cottage well removed from the busy Boston swirl? It would serve her well through the winter and into the spring.

I had almost no sleep that night, but it didn't matter, excited as I was to see her and share my thoughts. Alas, those thoughts would have to wait a while, since on this same morning a thick packet appeared in the Parker House mailroom, posted from Honolulu and tied with coconut twine. In the upper corner was a name I knew quite well. Lehua Pruitt was married to that cousin of mine who'd first introduced me to young Lydia Dominis on the French frigate's deck. He'd stayed in the islands, raised his family there, and made quite a bit of money in the shipping trade.

Lehua had known the Queen since childhood. Her weekly letters, like most coming from the islands, were written in Hawaiian, and these she would always answer herself, using the poetic code called *kaona,* a kind of word play built into the language, salting all messages, both spoken and written, with double and triple meanings. Take the Queen's name, the final syllables. *Lani* means sky. It also means heaven, and can refer to anything elevated—a tall mountain, a person of rank. This one word, as part of a name, links a chief or ruler to all things heavenly and divine.

When I dropped the day's bulging bundle on her parlor table, her hand went straight to this packet, grasping the edges as if it were a life preserver. She shook it and held it toward the window, as if some wintry light might pass through to reveal an outline of its contents.

"Dear Lehua. She has never abandoned me. She brought me food, you know, she brought me flowers, she sometimes bribed the guard to allow a little something extra, a jar of jam, a sweetcake."

"I wonder what she sends you now."

"I think I know."

"Something you've been expecting?"

"This is what I have been waiting for."

She untied the twine, peeled back the layers of wrapping, and drew forth first a letter, translating as she read.

"She says that all the orchids in my garden are flowering, the ones I planted before I left, and the rain has been light, just enough to keep them watered. This is good news, Julius, the best of news. I think I will soon be ready."

"Ready to..."

"To travel again."

"So soon?"

"I don't mean a great deal of travel, perhaps a very short trip."

"And where to, if I might ask?"

"I haven't quite decided. But I am hoping that you will join us."

"As you well know, Your Majesty, it would be my great honor, but...it would help to know where..."

"I'm sure we'll have that settled in a day or so."

"...and for how long."

"Yes, of course, and that would certainly depend upon where we go."

"England has been mentioned once or twice. But at this time of year..."

"No, nothing so adventurous as that."

Her lips opened in a cryptic smile, as if she were deliberately going around in circles. I tried not to show my impatience.

"Somewhere nearby, then? I know your cousins won't want you gone for long, when the weather can turn at a moment's notice."

"We may well return quite soon. I believe Joseph has taken the cottage for another week. So let us say it would be two or three days, four at the most. And your services, Julius, have become invaluable to me. I will pay you whatever is required."

"Pay? Pay? I beg your pardon, but I wouldn't hear of it!"

"Don't be silly..."

"If it's somewhere nearby, for merely a day or two or three...that is no time at all."

"It could be longer. I'm not quite sure until I think this through. Perhaps a week, surely no more than that."

"Well, even then. A week, two weeks...if it were nearby..."

"In your view, what would be a fair recompense?"

"No! No! No! No! This is out of the question!"

"I know you have other obligations."

"Nothing that cannot be attended to."

"I have the money. There is no shortage of money, at the moment."

My sleepless night was catching up with me. I almost raised my voice. Your Majesty, I almost said, this kind of waffling grows tedious! If you have a plan, just tell me what it is! Instead I said, "It's not about the money. It is...there are so many variables here. The length of time, the destination, the matter of clothing, what to prepare for..."

"Yes, forgive me. I'm being far too vague. Suppose then I simply pay you by the day. We'll agree on some sort of daily compensation, plus all expenses. Joseph is very good at these things. And you will continue to do what you have done so well, managing these hordes who seem to find us wherever we may be. Will you do it, Julius? It would make me very happy."

Her voice was incongruously seductive, seeming to contradict her words. I didn't know what to say. I thought she trusted me, but this evasiveness was the opposite of trust. I thought she wanted to stay put and get to work on the story she'd described with such urgency. To that end I'd let go of my literary dream. Now, less than twelve hours later, I had to let go of a second dream, her prolonged stay and a daily routine that would somehow sustain our common cause. Which is to say, I had to let go of *my* dream of what she should be doing next.

It was annoying. It was maddening, in fact, for a fellow of my disposition, fastidious to a fault, and very much set in my ways. Years earlier I would have relished the chance for an open-ended journey. But those days were long behind me, having reached an age when I craved certainty. And yet, in spite of myself, I knew I would surrender to her plea.

After all, what were my choices? To watch her ride away—for a day? or a week? or a month? or forever?—while I remained in the wintry confines of my ill-lit rooms, staring out the window at faceless men bundled in their scarves and overcoats hurrying up and down the broad steps of the Custom House? No, I'd done that once before and never ceased to regret it, let her slip past me, turned my back on an offer she seemed to be making, one that unsettled me and put old habits to the test, preferring to sail away toward the safety of this northern land. I was wiser, at least I thought I was, though no less fearful than I'd been in those early years. And fearful of what, you might ask? For now, call it the unknown.

In time I learned from Joseph that this twine-bound packet was the second she'd received. The first had reached her a week after they'd landed in San Francisco. She could have carried it from Honolulu but she knew her luggage would be searched and wanted nothing in hand that might delay her departure. She'd arranged for Lehua to send it by a later ship, addressed to the California Hotel.

After her parole she'd been granted the freedom of Oahu, though you could hardly call it freedom when her every move was monitored. To go anywhere else, to another island, or to go abroad, to leave the land she once had ruled, she had to request permission from the president of the new republic, a bearded patriarch descended from missionaries, a man, in my view, who should have been requesting permission from *her* to continue his life in those islands her people had inhabited for over two thousand years. She told him what she'd later tell the press: she only wanted a change of scene.

Apart from Joseph and Mrs. K and Lehua Pruitt, who were sworn to silence, she'd told no one else of her plans until the day before she left. Close friends were confused and bereft and stood tearful at the wharf to see her off. It was from the outset a journey of her own design, conceived in secret, by a woman who could not escape her celebrity yet moved with the wariness of an inmate recently released.

A STRANGE AND FATEFUL BOND

I take that back. This long journey was not entirely of her own design. Indeed, no one's is, indebted as we are to all the travelers who preceded us, whatever roads they may have followed. So it was with Lili'uokalani, her trip prefigured by other, older journeys years before her birth, by sailors and wanderers and pilgrims and zealots, opening up this improbable path to the city of Boston and beyond.

How did she come to have family ties so far from her island home, in a region so unlike her own? I may as well explain it now, before going any further, since this is a story in itself, so full of odd coincidence you might think it belonged in a work of fiction, perhaps in a rousing novel of maritime adventure—unless you knew something of the volume of traffic between New England and the Kingdom of Hawai'i, the whalers out of New Bedford and Nantucket, the China traders out of Newburyport, the vessels that had set forth year after year laden with Calvinist preachers, their

Bibles and their wives. As the brethren built their chapels and homes and schools and meeting halls, a fleet of ships continued to deliver hardware, kitchenware, foodstuffs, tools and furniture, the pianos and anvils and hinges and doorknobs and mirrors and rocking chairs and clocks that made our merchants wealthy.

It starts with a sea captain from southern Europe, a good-looking, ambitious fellow born in Trieste and raised in Italy, who dropped anchor here in 1819 with plans to immigrate and naturalize as an American citizen. Why? If pressed, Captain John Dominis would allude to a noble background that had grown burdensome and too confining, a claim made believable by his swarthy and aristocratic features. He liked what he'd heard about this new country, as a place where one could leave the past behind and start again. He already spoke passable English. He soon met and wooed and married one Mary Jones, the belle of a venerable Boston family. In time, between voyages, he would father two daughters and a son.

A restless man, he never lingered long in port. For fifteen years Captain Dominis plied between Massachusetts and the Pacific Ocean, voyages that took him to San Francisco Bay, the Columbia River, Sitka, Tokyo, Hong Kong, Manila, and several times to Hawai'i. Why he decided to move his family out there is still not clear. Perhaps he'd fallen for the place, as have any number of captains and ships' officers and deckhands. (I think of my mother's nephew, that cousin who'd first introduced me to Lydia Dominis; at an early age he'd gone to sea out of Salem, twice circled the world, and finally settled on Oahu, where he married his half-Hawaiian wife.) Or perhaps Captain John, having spent all those years crisscrossing our largest ocean, decided to reestablish himself right out in the middle of it.

When they made the move in 1837, his wife knew nothing about Hawai'i. Judging by her letters she was never content there. Surely it was hard to leave her homeland in midlife (she would have been thirty-five or so by then), to leave the extended family and head halfway around the globe. She had to part with her young daughters too, left behind to continue their schooling. But like the wives of the missionaries making this same grueling voyage around this same time, she was bound to follow her husband and so steeled herself for the long sail south past the Indies, Brazil, and Argentina, to the famously treacherous waters of the Cape, from there north again up the Chilean coast to Santiago and farther west, eighteen thousand miles in all. One can imagine what was going through Mary's mind when she first set eyes on Honolulu, in those days a sort of mid-ocean frontier town, with dirt roads, a walled fort beside the harbor, native grass houses intermixed with cottages and storefronts made of wood and coral block.

Eventually—again between voyages—the captain built her an elaborate compensation, a fine and sturdy replica of a prosperous country home, two stories, with pillars and porticoes and gardens. Alas, he never had a chance to enjoy the place. In 1846, the year it was to be finished, he'd sailed away again, on another voyage to China, this time in search of the elegant furnishings his wife deserved. He never returned. Presumably he died at sea. Perhaps foul play was involved. According to one ungrounded rumor passed on to me by the Queen, he was strangled in his sleep and his body thrown overboard. But by whom and for what reason was never clear. All reports are vague.

Also unclear is why Mary, now a widow in her forties with an adolescent son, remained in Hawai'i. After ten years Honolulu was still a rustic outpost compared with Boston, where she had a clan of landed relatives. Maybe she lacked the money for such a move and was too proud to admit it. Maybe it was too painful to return, her daughters having both died early. Perhaps she was now attached to the house she and her husband had worked for years to create, a symbol of whatever dreams they may have shared. Already a kind of Honolulu landmark, it was—and still is, fifty years later—one of the most admired buildings in the islands.

To make ends meet she took in boarders, the first being a U.S. commissioner to the kingdom. After the house was completed, he rented a suite of rooms and liked it so much he declared the Dominis home to be the American consulate. He raised our flag from a pole on the grounds and proposed that the house be named for George Washington so there would always be "a piece of American soil in Hawai'i!" Two years later he was recalled. Another commissioner arrived, the consulate moved to another part of town, and Washington Place was once again a private residence. But the name stuck, and the flag remained. Mary Jones Dominis kept it flying until the day she died, which I now take as a key to how she and many others of her era saw themselves and armored themselves.

For over fifty years this woman who would become the

Queen's mother-in-law dwelled in a foreign country, a sovereign kingdom with its own anthem and its own flag, yet in her heart she'd never left home. Again, one has to wonder what kept her in this remote land she regarded as a realm of exile. Had anyone forced her to stay? If she bore such allegiance to her native terrain, why didn't she return? And please don't misunderstand me here. This is not about the American flag. I love our flag, salute it with pride as often as I can. But there is a time and a place. I wonder how a British flag would have been received here in Boston had some English immigrant in the early days of our Republic insisted on flying the Union Jack above a Back Bay manor house for forty or fifty years?

As for young John Dominis, it must have shaped him, growing up the subject of a Hawaiian king in a house named for George Washington and presided over by a daily raising of the Stars and Stripes. You might say it was an intermingling that shaped them both, the sea captain's son and the young woman he would marry, both coming of age under two flags, two entangled histories.

Thanks to his determined mother, John, from boyhood onward, would often run with Hawaiians of the chiefly class. Mary didn't like them much, thought they lacked sound judgment, but in those days Hawaiians still governed their own nation, still had power and position and money and land. By the age of twenty-five he'd joined the staff of Prince Lot (later to inherit the throne). Lydia's first vivid memory of her husband-to-be comes from a day when they were riding on horseback side by side, among two hundred men and women in a royal traveling party. She was nineteen, and in her eyes John apparently struck a manly figure. Somehow he'd attained the rank of "General," though he'd never been to military school or seen combat. He cherished the title. It gave him reason to wear uniforms and sit tall in the saddle. Midway along their route, as they came to a narrow passage, an impatient rider tried to wedge his way between them. John, straining to rein his own horse aside, was thrown to the ground and broke his leg. Undaunted, he managed to lift himself onto the saddle and escort young Lydia home to her family's front door, where he dismounted and gallantly helped her down.

That was the day she noticed him, the day she remembered his earlier attentions. She let him continue to court her, and after a two-year engagement they were married, the wedding attended by everyone but John's mother. The king was there, a grandson of Kamehameha the Great, and all the high chiefs living on Oahu, for a ceremony conducted by the Reverend Samuel Damon, a Congregational minister known as "The Seaman's Friend." As for Mary Jones Dominis, she stood waiting with stern and unforgiving eyes in the parlor at Washington Place, caught in a web of her own design. While this marriage would surely secure John's chances for political advancement, Mary was not about to lose him to a dusky native woman, no matter how high-born she might be. She'd lost two daughters to the Boston winter and lost a husband to the hazards of the China Sea. John was all she had left.

For the next seven years Lydia would live with them in his mother's house, where Mary sabotaged any effort at domestic harmony. And yet she was the link to those thirty cousins the Queen would meet during her Boston visits, a tribe with holdings all around this town (more names and alliances, by the way, than I can claim to keep track of, having my own unwieldy clan to contend with, brothers and sisters and their proliferating offspring). From the family of Mary Jones they fan out now, cousins-by-marriage unto the second and third, perhaps fourth generation, chief among them the illustrious bookman, William Lee. A first cousin to the Queen's late husband, he is one of the few still living who actually remember John Dominis from his pre-Honolulu days. Sarah, his literary wife, would become a spiritual sister to the Queen, reaching out to her from the day they met.

These two are about the same age, share a love for books and poetry. And who knows? Is there some instinctive form of kinship, a subtle recognition between two women who have chosen first cousins as their mates, both drawn to some ancient feature in the lineage, a line of the jaw, or shading of the cheekbone, or slow dawning in the smile? For years they've corresponded, letters flowing between Brookline and Honolulu, always addressing each other as "My Dear Cousin." After the overthrow, Sarah took up the Hawaiian cause. With an illustrated lecture she began touring New England. She fought for the plight of a native people in a land she'd never seen and would never visit, propelled by her affection for the Queen, traveling from town to town, to church social halls and meetinghouses, like a gospel preacher on the revival circuit. She traces her lineage back to the Massachusetts Bay Colony, and at such times you can hear in her voice the Protestant generations behind her. You can see the pulpit style.

"I would never say a word against this grand country of ours," she declaims. "But I ask you, as Americans, if those faraway islands are going to be annexed, should we not first ask the Hawaiians themselves what they want? Should not a vote be taken?"

Here she will clutch the rostrum, her color will rise, a pink flush across the ivory cheeks. Her probing eyes will gleam as if with fever. "If we are a democratic people—if we truly believe in democracy!—before we claim their islands for ourselves, should we not at least allow them the right to vote on their own future?"

EVERYTHING STARTS WITH THE LAND

When we boarded the train it was snowing again, snowing all the way to Washington. The Hawaiians had seen so much snow they yielded to it, almost giddy at the prospect of an eternal winter. The entire world has turned to snow, said Joseph, and we will never see the earth again; from this day forward we will live like the Eskimo and travel everywhere by sled as we learned to do in Brookline.

At the Shoreham Hotel she had booked a corner suite for herself and Mrs. K, with separate rooms on either side, one for Joseph, one for me. There'd been no announcement of her departure. Until we reached the Park Square Station I myself didn't know where we were bound. ("Rest assured," she told me. "We won't be going anywhere outside the country, not for the time being.") There were no reporters on the train nor any to greet us as we disembarked. Yet somehow the word got out. Perhaps the bell captain mentioned to a hack driver that Her Majesty had just checked in, and perhaps this driver mentioned it to his next fare, who mentioned it to her sister, who happened to be married to a State Department clerk who met for beers on Friday with an old school chum, now a copyeditor with the *Washington Post*...

By the next afternoon I was fending off queries from the *Post* and the *Washington Star* and bureau chiefs from Philadelphia and Baltimore and New York. Once cards began to pile up at the main desk the Queen had them all passed on to me. "Please tell them, Julius, that I can't speak with anyone right now. Tell them to come back next Tuesday, when we will receive all members of the press here in my suite between three and five."

I'd brought along my typewriter. Outside my door I posted a sign:

HER MAJESTY'S PRESS SECRETARY
Please Knock

The ones who found me asked the same questions they'd asked in Boston. And I had to give out the same answers. She is here on a social visit, with no official role. How long she'll be staying is hard to say. Which was true. I'm sure she herself did not yet know, having booked our rooms for one week. As for me, I still had no clear idea why we were there, not until her intentions at last began to emerge on our third day in town, a Monday, when she asked Joseph and me to deliver a message to the White House.

It was three blocks from the hotel, an easy walk once the snow stopped falling, under wintry skies of an icy and sparkling blue, and it occurred to me then that the Shoreham may not have been a random choice.

We were met by the president's personal secretary, who

received our cards with a guarded look at Joseph, probably assuming he was a Negro. He may have recognized my name, since I'd been there a time or two on assignment, though his half-smile was unreadable. A sentinel in morning coat at the gate of the castle, he informed us that Monday wasn't a day when President Cleveland received visitors, nor was it a day when he welcomed messages of any type. When I told him we brought personal greetings from Queen Lili'uokalani, showing him the blue-bordered envelope, her name engraved, the stiffness in his body dissolved. He blinked, accepting it with a kind of reverence, and said he'd do his best to deliver it right away.

I half expected he would pocket it awhile and let Cleveland have his day of executive peace and quiet. She'd sent him the simplest kind of note, not from a former head of state to a current head of state, but closer to what might pass between two longtime acquaintances. She was in town, it said, and if he ever had a free moment she'd be pleased to make an informal call. By the time Joseph and I had ambled back to the Shoreham, this same secretary had sent a handwritten reply. The president would be pleased to receive her at 3 p.m. that afternoon.

I was astonished. She was not, seeming to expect nothing less. She already knew what she would wear: the fur-collared winter coat, the woolen hat in the Russian style, her red and orange feather lei.

I have puzzled over the quickness of this response from Grover Cleveland, known to be a workhorse who put in long hours at his desk. I now trace it back to their first meeting some ten years earlier, when she and then-queen Kapi'olani were en route to London for Victoria's Golden Jubilee. After their stop in Boston, they'd come down to Washington for a state visit, highlighted by a White House banquet, a glittering and sumptuous affair under chandeliers. Cleveland, halfway through his first term, had seated the Queen at his right hand, while at his left sat Princess Lili'uokalani, the king's sister. She was there to translate for the sister-in-law who spoke no English. The first queen of any land to visit the United States, Kapi'olani, alas, was out of her element, never comfortable in such gatherings, a diffident woman, sweet-hearted and shy.

The affable Cleveland, at ease with his great girth and generally pleased with himself, having recently, at forty-nine, married a gorgeous woman less than half his age, made every effort to chat with his guest of honor. In the end, he spent much of the evening tilting away from her and attending to the Princess, who not only spoke impeccable English but had come dressed in a low-cut gown of black velvet accented with embroidery and black lace at the bodice. Her raven hair coiled in a French twist and fixed with a silver comb, she seemed to glory in the chatter and the glow. Her husband, John, traveling with the royal party, had missed the dinner, sent his regrets, and stayed in their hotel room, claiming excessive fatigue and a flare-up of chronic rheumatism. Perhaps his absence freed her to release the full measure of her charm, still youthful, yet more imperious, I would say, more forceful than in the days when I first knew her. For eight months, while her brother, King David Kalakaua, toured the world, she'd taken his place to rule as Regent of the Kingdom, and was now appointed heir-apparent. Unlike her sister-in-law, the well-coifed Princess could voice strong opinions, she could laugh at witty remarks and make some of her own. Lit by candelabra spaced along the endless table, her eyes flashed with wise merriment, and Cleveland, known to have a taste for the ladies, would not forget her, beguiled, as I had been beguiled on the night we met. And in time she would call on him, as she eventually called on me.

A year later, when he ran for reelection, he lost to Benjamin Harrison, a Republican from Indiana, in every way the opposite of Cleveland, austere, aloof, known by his staff as "the human iceberg." Unlike Cleveland, the new president favored expansion into the Pacific and the annexation of Hawai'i and, toward the end of his term, tacitly sanctioned the overthrow. Within two weeks after the Queen was ousted, a commission from Honolulu had rushed to the capitol—seven attorneys and businessmen—to seize the day, lobbying hard and fast. And they nearly succeeded. As Harrison's final act he sent to the Senate a lopsided annexation treaty that required no vote by the people of Hawai'i, only ratification by Congress and by the hastily established, all-white "Provisional Government," which claimed to be in control of the islands. It might have passed, had not Grover Cleveland come to the rescue.

In 1892 he had run again, this time defeating Harrison in a landslide. Sure that she had an ally in the president-elect, the deposed Queen straightaway sent off a letter to "My great and good friend..." Refusing to submit to the Missionary Boys, she chose instead to give the United States a chance to make things right:

> I feel comforted (she wrote to Cleveland) that I have the boon of your personal friendship and goodwill.... I beg that you will give your friendly assistance in

> granting redress for a wrong which we claim has been done to us, under the color of the assistance of the naval forces of the United States in a friendly port…

To Cleveland's everlasting credit, he was appalled. As his first presidential act, five days after taking the oath of office, he removed Harrison's treaty from the table, pending a full investigation. When he appeared before the joint members of Congress to voice his personal dismay and outrage, Cleveland outdid himself. I was there in the press gallery to cover it, to witness his amplitude spilling past the podium, his voice quivering at times, his great jowls alive with indignation.

"If a feeble but friendly state is in danger of being robbed of its independence and its sovereignty by the misuse of the name and power of the United States, the United States cannot fail to vindicate its honor and its sense of justice by an earnest effort to make all possible reparation…"

Now four more years had passed. Once again she found herself in Washington, with the future of her homeland still undecided, and Cleveland had rearranged his afternoon.

She hired a carriage, to be seen arriving in style, insisting that all three of us come along. At times like this she has a way of setting her shoulders and lifting her chin. She mounted the stairs of the north portico as if she owned the place, striding past the dozen reporters who stood waiting, scribbling away. I knew most of them and again wondered how they'd got wind of this on such short notice—while they were wondering how I came to be marching past them and into the interior of the presidential mansion in the company of this entourage from Polynesia.

Kinkaid was there, having hurried down from Boston over the weekend, sure now that he'd been right to probe the political agenda.

"Hello Bobby," I said, "didn't expect to see you today."

"And likewise, Julius," flashing his crooked and irreverent smile. "You've come a long way for a stringer."

"Just doing my job."

"Come now. What gives? Don't tell me this is old home week."

"We'll issue a statement as soon as we can."

"Right you are. Next thing we know you'll be running for office."

Doors opened ahead of us and we were ushered at last into an intimate salon called the Red Room, lushly carpeted, with carved wood furnishings, against one wall an upright piano. As the president's secretary closed the door, a hush fell over us. Ever the sentinel, he stood nearby, next to a young intern eagerly taking notes. We three were seated off to the side, Joseph and Mrs. K and me, on upholstered chairs, just as Cleveland made his entrance.

He's a huge man, weighing close to three hundred pounds, his broad, polished forehead made broader by receding hair which apparently has reappeared as a thick, brushy moustache angling past his lips. His swollen bulk loomed above the Queen, yet did not overwhelm her. She stood her ground, seemed to grow an inch or two as he grasped her outstretched hand with both of his, a rosy flush across his cheeks, the glisten of moisture in his eyes.

"I'm so very glad to see you. How kind and generous to think of calling. You have often been in my thoughts..."

"As you have been in mine. I'm touched that you found some time on such a busy day."

"Nonsense. It's a day made brighter by this surprise."

He glanced at us, and she said, "Please meet my staff."

As she spoke our names he nodded. "You are all most welcome, and most fortunate too, to be accompanying this grand lady."

He lightly held her elbow, guiding her to a sofa by the window, and they began to talk as if somehow alone in that crowded room, first exchanging pleasantries—the weather, his wife and daughter, what brings her to the capital. I was struck by the ease with which she drew him to her, coming there not as a supplicant but as a woman with the right to such an audience, calling forth an old gallantry and in his eyes a look any man would recognize, that reigniting of a spark.

"And tell me now," he asked, "how do your people fare? In these past four years, have they been treated well, I mean, treated civilly?"

"I wish I could say yes. In truth, they feel excluded now, ruled by a government they did not choose. Their very language is in danger. English will soon be used in all the schools. It is to be an official policy. Think what it would mean if your language were taken away."

He winced, as if stabbed with a long pin, and she hastened to add, "I should also tell you your name is very dear to the Hawaiian people. In my own heart I always hold a place for you and what you said, for your effort to do what was just, when no one else would raise a voice."

She touched his sleeve, and again bright color tinted his

fleshy cheeks. "I did what I could, I honestly believe I did."

"We know you did."

It should be noted that his opposition to the overthrow and to the illegal use of our fleet marines had been delivered not only to Congress but to the Missionary Boys themselves, in the strongest terms, ordering them to reinstate the Queen. And how did they receive it? They defied him! From their offices in Honolulu they sent back a fifty-page reply saying, in effect, We are in control, we're Hawaiian too, we were born here and have finally rid ourselves of an outworn royal charade. If you want to restore an ill-equipped, inept, and self-serving woman to her tinpot throne, then you must come out and do so by force of arms. We have our own militia now, a few hundred able-bodied sharpshooters who are willing to make a stand for the American way of life.

Again to Cleveland's credit, he was willing to go that far to squash their outlaw insurgency, to erase what he saw as a stain upon his nation's honor. If only Congress had backed him up! But they wouldn't approve the money. Sending troops and warships on such a long and dubious campaign was too risky, and too costly. In those days they didn't have much money, still teetering as we were on the brink of bankruptcy, the entire country, thanks to that ill-conceived scheme to replace the gold standard with silver. (It was a scheme Cleveland had inherited, by the way, devised to buy support from mining barons in the Far West.) For the men in Washington, straining to salvage their own careers, the Pacific Ocean and its squabbles seemed suddenly too far away. In the end Cleveland had to settle for a hands-off policy, declaring it had never been America's business to meddle in another country's internal affairs. And Lili'uokalani had been left to fend for herself.

She blamed Congress. She blamed Harrison and his inner circle. But she didn't blame Cleveland. She had forgiven him, her brown hand upon his sleeve a small gesture for a large forgiveness for transgressions both known and as yet unknown. For an instant he had the look of a penitent who knows his slate has just been cleared. She possessed that quality, as if offering a kind of papal absolution. She could also pronounce a curse that would one day make my scalp crawl. She had that in her too.

Now she reached into a handsome bag made of Chinese silk. As she drew forth two thin folders bound in leather, his great brow furrowed with curiosity.

"I bring you something from Honolulu. I hope you will have time to read it very soon."

"If it comes from you, I will read it before the day is gone."

"As you may know, my people still look to you as one who recognizes their struggle."

"Well, Your Majesty, I am gratified to hear that, though surely they understand, and you understand, that my time here is running short..."

His voice trailed off. Having opened the first folder, he had begun scanning its pages. As I would soon learn, these were from the packet sent by Lehua Pruitt a week after the Queen reached San Francisco, a long petition, one version in Hawaiian, one in English. Here, in brief, is what it said:

> The people of Hawai'i still trust the government of the United States, a trust that reaches back more than

> fifty years to 1843, when the United States formally recognized the independence of their kingdom.
>
> Once again we are asking President Cleveland that the monarchy unjustly taken from us by persons who claim to represent the United States be restored. This restoration would undo the wrong done to us and return to us our Queen, to whom, by our own constitution as well as by our choice, we have a perfect right.
>
> This plea is in keeping with the only instructions given to those who established the so-called Republic of Hawaiʻi, the words of President Cleveland himself, when he acknowledged "the right of the Hawaiian people to choose their own form of government."
>
> In the meantime, Liliʻuokalani has the full power to represent the people of Hawaiʻi and to act in any way her judgment should dictate for the good of the Hawaiians.

He raised his eyes, blinking with what looked like remorse. "As things stand now, I'm sure you know that bringing back your monarchy is simply not possible."

She nodded. "As things stand now. But if our islands are not annexed, if that can be avoided, people will then demand a chance to vote on their future. I bring this petition to inform you of their deepest desire. They know how much you have already done, simply by removing President Harrison's treaty..."

"Nothing else made sense to me. And I'm proud to say that during my entire term it has not come up again, no more bills of any kind, though the talk of annexation never seems to end. It ebbs and flows like the tide, and now they say another commission will soon arrive from Honolulu to twist the arm of my successor."

"Do you think he will listen?"

"I doubt it. Certainly not before a vote is taken in Hawai'i. He strikes me as a democratic man."

"That is what makes them tremble."

"You mean the vote?"

"Those who claim to govern us say they believe in democracy. But this is the last thing they want. If my people are truly allowed to speak their minds, all of them, they will vote to be ruled once again by Hawaiians."

"I have so few days left, scarcely a month. But I will do what I can, I promise you. In the meantime I'm so pleased that we had this chance."

"One more thing. I want you to know about those who send this petition. As you can see, Patriotic League is their English name. But that does not tell you enough. The Hawaiian name tells you more. *Hui Aloha 'Aina.* Hui is a club or a group. 'Aina is the land, the earth, the soil, and also the place on earth you belong to. This is what you need to know about Hawaiians. Everything starts with the land beneath their feet. They love their land as you love yours."

"So tell me the name again?"

"Hui Aloha 'Aina. An Alliance of Those Who Love and Revere Our Place on Earth."

Again he took her hand in his and for a few moments they sat on the sofa like former lovers meeting for what they both knew would probably be the last time. I confess to a pang of envy, seeing new moisture rising into his eyes, and into hers, envy mixed with an upwelling of comradely affection for this enormous fellow who was both President of the United States and an ordinary man with some heat in his blood.

At last he said, "You are a brave and noble woman."

"And you, sir, will never be forgotten by the people of Hawai'i."

I wanted to be Cleveland then, sitting beside her on a plush sofa in the Red Room of the White House, hands entwined, saying I would do all I could. And if I were president, what would that mean? What might I *not* be able to achieve in the month remaining to me? Four years earlier, when this term began, Cleveland had taken less than a week to bury Harrison's treaty and stonewall the Missionary Boys.

ANOTHER KIND OF STORY

We followed an usher to the outer hall where the gaggle of reporters still waited, notebooks in hand.

"Your Majesty," one fellow called out, with a respectful nod, "is there time for just a few brief questions?"

"Your Majesty," called another, "will you be staying for the inauguration?"

This was Bobby Kinkaid, perhaps thinking he had an advantage, hoping she'd remember him from her first night in Boston. And maybe she did. She looked at me. I raised my arm.

"The Queen will receive all members of the press in her suite tomorrow, Tuesday, from three to five."

We tried to step past them, heading for the staircase, step past their unabashed fascination with fallen royalty, past all their suspicious eyes trained on me, the one writer privy to a meeting they'd hungered to witness. Kinkaid grabbed my passing sleeve.

"Julius, dear boy, we can't really wait that long. Today is no ordinary day…"

I saw that he was right and from his mocking eyes saw that, like the president's secretary, I was taking myself far too seriously. While Joseph escorted the Queen and Mrs. K, I lingered to field their questions, knowing they'd already noted her costume, the carriage, the time elapsed, knowing too they had no choice but to run with my account. It would have been easy to lord it over them, since whatever I said would become the official version, to be published Tuesday in all the D.C. papers, in St. Louis, Chicago, Baltimore, and New York. I strove for a chummy and fraternal tone, telling them it had been nothing more than a personal reunion. I summed up most of their remarks, with no mention made of the long message from Hui Aloha 'Aina. That was between Cleveland and the Queen.

By keeping those folders out of the news, you see, I hoped to serve her desire to be seen as a tourist. Yet even if that were so, if this trip were purely recreational, her very presence in the city was widely viewed as a strategic maneuver of some kind or another.

Hankering for answers, ready to hear more from the Queen herself, the entire press corps turned out on the following afternoon, dozens of reporters and stringers and bureau chiefs and feature writers, only to find themselves outnumbered by a throng that filled the corridors of the second floor. The whole town, it seemed, had heard that she was "receiving." Women who kept rooms there sent down their cards and queries, just as they'd done in Boston. But the Shoreham had a somewhat different clientele. Close to the White House, close to the executive offices, it was often used by congressmen and their wives. Did she know this in advance? I'm still not sure. She didn't hesitate to invite them all, anyone with press credentials, anyone then registered at the hotel, as well as anyone with a tie to government, along with their wives and daughters, since cards had also been sent from various department heads hoping to get a glimpse, perhaps a brief audience while she was still in their midst.

It was my job to stand at the door of her suite and receive their cards, allow them in or not allow them (curious citizens would wander in out of the cold and have to be turned away, and a few friends of friends who'd tagged along), and then to make the proper introductions:

"Your Majesty, may I present Mr. Warren Peabody from the *Baltimore Sun*..."

"Your Majesty, it is my pleasure to present Mrs. George Perkins, whose husband, as you may recall, is a senator from California..."

This was new to me, and I confess it was a satisfying role, the little rush of power each time I granted entrance to the inner sanctum. And yet I felt betrayed. Did she not understand that I'd promised these correspondents a meeting at such and such a time? She wanted me there to intercede, but how could my credibility survive? Or hers?

One by one they were stepping past me into a suite packed with well-wishers, Her Majesty surrounded, her hair well-coifed, wearing pearls, a low-cut gown, shaking hands, welcoming everyone, her black eyes flashing, ignited by the festive mood. To my surprise the world-weary reporters didn't seem to mind, as if they too were ready for a party on this blustery afternoon, or perhaps ready to settle for another kind of story.

Kinkaid was among the last to arrive, his surly eyes regarding me. "And so, dear boy, do I meet your standards? Or must I lurk here in the hallway and peek through the door like a lost urchin peeking through the gates?"

"Bobby, you are most welcome. But the Queen, alas, is not going to be as forthcoming as we had hoped."

"Hoped, indeed. And yet she seems quite talkative. Perhaps I can skulk around her circle there and do some covert eavesdropping. Would that be taking advantage? Off the record, as they say?"

He scanned the room, his lips agitating toward a tilted grin, while in his voice I heard a softer, less caustic note.

"My, my! Correct me if I'm wrong, but she has changed, you know, since that gathering on Christmas night. I see it now quite clearly, as you must too. The way she works the room. Look there! She knows exactly what she's doing. And these ladies, these Washington wives, they love her. You can be sure they'll be talking to their husbands later on. She is unique, she is exotic. And yet…and yet she can be one of them. It is quite remarkable how she gives the lie to all those sniping malcontents in the newsrooms of this nation who speak of her 'dark eminence,' who call her 'The Pickaninny Princess.' Just today that scurrilous editorial in the *Washington Times* refers to her as 'the sometime chieftainess of a cannibal family.' The writer, by the way, is here among us at this very moment, a shameless fellow who will mock the Queen and then help himself to her generous fare. See him there by the far window reaching for yet another tidbit. And surely each bite goes down with a taste of guilt as he finally observes her at close range, the way she handles herself—each gesture, each glance, the assurance, the joie de vivre. Whatever else may come of this visit, she will be seen as an ambassador, Julius, an elegant ambassador for those islands you're so fond of."

I'd never expected to hear anything like this from the mouth of Kinkaid. No sarcasm had leavened these words. I looked at him carefully and looked again at the Queen, seeing that he was right. Sooner or later Kinkaid is always right.

When he turned to me again the mischief had come back to his eyes. "And what about you, dear boy? What's your role in all this?"

"As you can see, it is modified from day to day."

"We already miss you up in Boston, you know. Will you be returning to us soon? Or are you now permanently attached to this retinue? Some say you have become indispensable now, as the confidant…or perhaps, if you'll pardon the expression, as a consort of sorts, as has been bandied about in certain circles."

"Hold on now, Kinkaid! What is that supposed to mean?"

He shrugged.

"Which circles?" I said.

"You might say those same sly and sniping malcontents who are always jumping to bizarre conclusions."

Sudden heat came rising into my neck and face. "They can put those rumors to rest right now!"

"Don't take offense."

"The Queen and I are colleagues, Bobby, nothing more!"

"Well, of course, dear boy. It goes without saying. I'll just slide away now and do some mingling on my own."

A NAMELESS CALLER

"Confidant," he said, and his insinuating tone gave it a covert ring, as if the Queen and I were conspirators in some illicit scheme. Yet I didn't mind that, not at all, considering the many ways she'd taken me into her confidence.

"Consort" was another matter, the word itself causing my voice to lift a notch or two in protest. And why, you might ask, what's wrong with "consort"? Doesn't it mean a partner, an associate, a fellow traveler? Well yes, there's that. But the word has another layer, hinting at a sweeter kind of closeness, in the royal sense, that rare intimacy granted to the spouse of a reigning queen. "Prince Consort"—this had been Albert's title, late husband of Victoria, the trusted advisor, ever at her side. Up to a point, you might say, my role was becoming much like his. But only up to a point. And this was precisely why Kinkaid's allusion goaded me, reminding me what I was *not,* what we were *not,* though the world might see it otherwise: by her side in Boston, spending most of each day at her cottage, now protocol officer and public companion, with rooms on the same floor of the same hotel, etc., etc.

We'd been there less than a week and already rumors were in the air, with new questions added to the mix. How long is she staying? What is she really doing here? Was that spur-of-the-moment call on our lame duck president the sum of her intentions? And what in God's name is going on between this so-called Queen and her so-called secretary? What sort of Hawaiian hanky-panky have they imported to our fair city?

As veiled innuendoes crept onto the editorial pages, I thought at first my duty would be to shield the Queen, perhaps by issuing a denial—"Despite all reports to the contrary..."—but denials only raise more questions. With rumors like these, there is no setting the record straight. The more press you get, the more press you get. Say nothing then. Sit still and ride it out—a lesson the Queen had learned long ago. She was past the need for shielding. In Honolulu for years her enemies had circulated stories of liaisons with the household help, with gardeners, with a half-Tahitian bodyguard, always under titillating headlines: "More Palace Intrigue," "Her Majesty's Imperiled Virtue." I know now she'd had lovers, but never those so self-righteously singled out by columnists. "I don't read the papers anymore," she told me once, with a wise and melancholy smile. "Knowing what they've said about me, how can I trust what they say about anyone else?"

The next couple of weeks did nothing to dispel such gossip. A record snowfall had descended upon the city, the side streets piling high with drifts. Holed up behind closed doors, none of us left the Shoreham for days at a time.

> Has the Queen's party moved on (asked the *Washington Times*), slipping away in the dead of night? Or are they merrily laying low, snug and cozy at their exotic ease? Only the desk clerk knows for sure.

I for one gave thanks for the weather. With no clue yet as to what she might do next, I'd been braced to set off again at a moment's notice (some of my shirts were still unpacked) for England, for New York, for San Francisco or back to Boston. Now she booked rooms for a second week, and then for a third, and I was caught somewhere between surrender and security, willing to be guided by her next impulse or whatever one might choose to call it—whim, intuition, inspiration, a still-to-be-revealed campaign—yet much relieved to sit tight a while, forced by the elements to stay put, to find a routine in the slow pattern of February days, thinking that one of these afternoons the time might come to open up her notes and begin to move the story of her life along its path. Before we left I'd mentioned this book idea to Sarah Lee, whose editorial eyes filled with high purpose. "Oh Julius!" she exclaimed. "What a great gift that would be! We must all do whatever we can! The sooner the better!"

And it might have gone that way. Who knows? We might still be taking rooms at the Shoreham, were it not for the series of messages that now came toward us like dark seabirds riding the advance of a wintry wind.

Coverage of her visit had led to another surge of mail from near and far. Once again our snowed-in mornings were given to sifting through it all, letter by letter, card by card—a congressman's wife upstairs inviting her to tea, an undersecretary inviting her to tour the Justice Department, a breeder from Louisville, Kentucky, saying he'd named a horse for her and expected it to win the Derby.

On a day when the streets and skies were white and still, laden with expectation, there came a telegram from San Francisco, not part of the stack I'd carried up from the mailroom, but delivered an hour or so later by a bellboy bearing a yellow Western Union envelope.

Without glancing away from the letter in her hand she said, "Is it for you or me?"

"It's for you. Shall I open it?"

"Yes, go ahead. Who would be sending me a telegram?"

"It's all in Hawaiian."

She looked up then, pushing the spectacles onto her forehead, with a nod of pleasure that said she knew who'd sent it. "I'd better take a look at this."

I passed the page and watched that pleasure drain from her face.

"Bad news?"

She studied the words, blinking, thinking, before she slowly began to translate.

"Aloha, Lili'u…They say a shark is in the shallow water… smelling blood…Lehua knows the story. Be on guard."

I waited, not wanting to voice what I knew it meant.

At last she said, "They may be sending someone to kill me. I will know more when I receive Lehua's letter."

"They? They? Who is they?"

"You know as well as I do, Julius."

"Someone from where? Honolulu? The West Coast?"

Remarkably calm, she said, "We will wait for Lehua's letter."

"That could be a week or more! I'm going downstairs to alert security, and then let the police know. The station is a block from here."

She took my hand. "Please sit down, Julius. No need to call in the police. Not yet."

"What do you mean, 'not yet'?"

She settled back, pushed the spectacles up into her hair, and told me this was not the first such warning. In Brookline, every week or so a note would arrive sounding the alarm, begging her to be careful for her life. But she was used to this. It had been going on for years, threats of every type, signs of danger sometimes real, sometimes imagined by an overly protective ally who'd heard a story from someone else who'd heard a story. She shared today's news with me, she said, because Lehua had a level head and her husband knew everyone.

Four days later the letter appeared, half in code, half a scattered assemblage of names and sailing times and a friend's gushing sentiment. Who the assassin would be, how or when he would arrive, Lehua wasn't sure, writing in haste, she said, so as not to miss the next ship bound for California, the same ship that would carry Hawaii's Attorney General across the water, on his way to Washington, D.C.

Once the Queen had deciphered it all, a sequence became quite clear. Word of her presence in the capital had quickly made its way back home—a telegram to San Francisco from the office of Hawaii's U.S. Minister, and from there by ship. The news reached Honolulu just as the new delegation of lobbyists was about to set off in our direction, bearing yet another annexation treaty, intending to lay it before William McKinley as soon as he took office. And now look what had happened! The renegade Queen had deceived them, her stop in Boston but a ploy. She'd already been admitted to the Red Room. Influential wives were rallying to her cause. Her stay in the capital was sure to be a great embarrassment, if not a hindrance to any serious negotiations with the new president, since many there still regarded her as a legitimate head of state, or wanted to, or were willing to hear her side of the story. In Honolulu her opponents were blaming one another for ever letting her out of their sight. According to Lehua Pruitt, the more virulent among them would now like to silence that story once and for all.

* * *

Later that same night a knock roused me. I had just dozed off, and tried to ignore it but there came a louder, more insistent rapping at the door.

"Who is it?"

"Begging your pardon, sir, but it's a long-distance call."

"From where?"

"New York City."

"Is it for me?"

"It's for Her Majesty, but she doesn't answer, sir."

"I'll be right there."

In robe and slippers I rushed out and tried her room again, rapping repeatedly. "Your Majesty! A call from New York!"

This time the sleepy voice called back, "Please take it, Julius. I'm not dressed to go downstairs."

Neither was I, a ridiculous spectacle, my bathrobe wrapped around rumpled pajamas. Thankfully, apart from the young night clerk, the lobby was empty. The long-distance booth stood next to his desk. As the D.C. operator connected me I leaned in close to the mouthpiece.

"Hello?"

No answer.

I shouted, "Who's calling?"

A man said, "I want to speak with Lydia Dominis," the voice so frail, so distant it seemed to be coming from two thousand miles away.

"I can take the message."

"I have to speak with her."

"It's almost eleven. She doesn't want to be disturbed."

"And who are you?"

"Her secretary. What's this about?"

The line sputtered.

"Can you hear me?" I shouted. "You still there?"

His voice was so thin, so prickled with static I couldn't tell if he was friend or foe.

"Mrs. Dominis has three days to get out of Washington, D.C. If she stays any longer her life won't be worth a nickel."

"Who is this?"

"Did you hear what I said?"

"I need to know who I'm talking to."

"It doesn't matter. Just tell her what I said."

"Where did you get that information?"

"I'm not at liberty to say."

"What's your name?"

"I don't have a name."

Again the voice receded, blurred with static. A click, and the line went dead.

At that hour the clerk also ran the hotel switchboard. He was new to the equipment but finally put me through to the same operator, who told me she could reconnect me with New York but not with the man who'd called unless I had a number.

Back upstairs I tried her door, calling out, "Your Majesty!" until it opened a crack and her face was there.

"What's the matter?"

"I know it's late, but this is urgent."

She studied my face. "It's another message," she said.

"Yes."

"Just a moment, then."

She closed the door and a minute later opened it, wrapped in a loose dressing gown. "Come in. But please speak quietly," with a nod toward the bedroom of Mrs. K and her nasal snore.

Moving to the sofa, she gestured for me to join her there. As I told her what I'd heard she nodded, once again seeming not at all troubled by the news, as if she'd been expecting it, as if she'd known all along it was only a matter of time before the world she'd left behind caught up with her.

When I said I'd call on the White House first thing in the morning, to ask for some kind of protection, she almost laughed. That is, I thought I saw her smile, though in the half-light it was hard to tell, her face shaded, partially obscured by her hair, which hung loose. When she began to speak, her voice was low and soothing, adding to the eerie nature of that moment. Though we were sitting where we sat most mornings, going through the mail, it had become a different room, somewhere outside of time, as we sat side by side in the near-dark, both wrapped in our night clothes, I in my pajamas, she in her gown, with black hair falling past her shoulders.

"I haven't told you, Julius, that this very kind of threat came to me three times while I was staying at Washington Place. After the overthrow I had no idea what would become of me. Three times I was warned that if I tried to restore my monarchy I would not live to resume the throne. I was waiting then to hear a response from President Cleveland, and I was terrified. I knew not what to do. And yet time slowly passed, and I was still alive, and threats like those continued for the next five years. I know now that they had many chances to kill me. If they truly wanted to, wouldn't it have been simpler to do it there, on Oahu? Far simpler than sending someone all the way out here."

"I'm not so sure about that," I said. "In these eastern cities it might be easier for an agent to come and go, easier to disappear. Honolulu is such a small town, even now, with few secrets. Everyone there knows everything."

She leaned toward me to tell me a story as Hawaiians are wont to do late at night when low light and muted voice can give every recollection the flavor of a ghostly folktale.

"They don't have the stomach for it. I will tell you how I know this. When my brother was king he too received many threats against his life. He lived in constant fear. Ten years ago some of the same men who now control the government hatched a plan to finish him off. They wanted to rewrite our constitution so that whites would have more control over everything; he was in their way. They were afraid he wouldn't sign it. They drew straws. Whoever drew the shortest straw would carry out the deed and shoot the king. But the one who drew the shortest straw couldn't do it. He didn't have it in him, so their plan fell through.

"I know that man. He grew up on Kauai, where his father did missionary work. It is the softest island, you know, in its spirit. In some ways he is a very soft-hearted man, with a wife and children. I know his wife. He is now the president of what they call the Republic, the same man who gave me permission to leave Oahu in December. I had to plead with him to let me travel, and in his eyes I saw the guilt he carries to this day. He knows that I know he once plotted to kill my brother. Perhaps as a way to make amends he let me leave and take the ship to California, and you can be sure he regrets it now. Friends and critics alike are blaming him—this is what Lehua says—arguing back and forth about what to do."

For a while we did not speak, the mood somehow deepened by Mrs. K's steady snoring from beyond the bedroom door, like lines of rolling distant surf. She watched me, as if testing my reaction, and I was thinking of a time when I would have agreed with her, since I too knew this man. In the months before the overthrow I'd interviewed him twice, a tall, civil fellow with a white-bearded Old Testament dignity, who seemed uncomfortable in his role as a revolutionary, as if he'd somehow been talked into it by others. A year later, when I returned to cover her trial, I saw with my own eyes what he and his cohorts had resorted to in the name of law and order. In the wake of an uprising against their authority, Honolulu had become a prison ruled by fear, where columns of young Hawaiian men shuffled through the streets linked by ball and chain, their only crime an unswerving loyalty to the woman who once had been their high chief and queen.

"Perhaps," I said at last, "there was a time when they stopped short. But hasn't everything changed? You know far better than I how desperate they've become, with so much of the populace against them. I fear that now they will stop at nothing."

She shook her head. As she reached up to touch a loosened lock of hair, her robe fell open at the top, revealing flesh she did nothing to conceal, eager to tell another story that had become a legend, her voice both gentler and fuller, almost not her own, as if someone now spoke through her.

"Some say they want to kill me, while others say not yet. But all of it is talk, because there is something else they know, men like him, born in the islands. They may profess to be Christians and look down their noses at the native way. But they have all heard what can happen if you harm someone of royal blood. They know that from olden times it is *kapu*. They know what happened to America's foreign minister after he allowed the marines to come ashore from the warship in the harbor and surround our palace and force me out. They know that a week later the same minister's daughter fell into the water and drowned while she was boarding the inter-island steamer."

I knew this story. In Honolulu, among those who wished for the downfall of the Missionary Boys and all those with a part in the overthrow, it was told and retold like a parable passed along from age to age. Yet the Queen had made it new, sitting as still as a sage, speaking with an oracle's voice, a deep-throated pronouncement that said she could trust this old *kapu* to protect her, even from six thousand miles away.

I didn't believe in curses, or didn't want to, certainly didn't want to rely on one for her safety. In my valise I kept a small pistol and decided then, as we sat in our bedclothes, at midnight on the second floor of the Shoreham Hotel, that I would load it and carry it with me on every outing.

"Once," I said, "I interviewed the captain of that steamer. He told me that on the Big Island, where she drowned, there are certain coves too rocky for a small craft to come ashore, so passengers are sometimes loaded onto the ship from above, by basket. In fact, I mention this in one of my dispatches. The captain said that in the best of times it's a precarious maneuver."

"Yes, I have heard that too. It may well have been an accident. Or perhaps God's will. But it happened nonetheless, a week after the minister's crime. And they all know it happened. They all know the daughter was in good health. It was broad daylight too. And there was no storm or strong wind or heavy surf that day to make the water rough."

She shrugged, and with that shrug her body relaxed, her own voice came back into the room.

"I'm glad you're here, Julius. Thank you for taking that call."

She was the Queen again, and her generous smile said, "Bear with me," a suddenly sweet and welcoming smile, though her dark eyes were still making predictions.

Her hand reached out then, to rest on mine, and in an instant the years fell away. Our entire world had changed. Yet nothing had changed. She was fifty-eight, and she was twenty-nine, the same eyes, same hair, now laced with silver, same smile, same melodious voice that had held me captive during the weeks and months that followed our meeting in the moonlit harbor. For a split second the walls around us fell away, winter melted, and we were this close together on a beach at sundown in a salty breeze off the water. Her hand rests on my arm, and she has just told me a cautionary tale with this same look, a generous smile somehow at odds with her eyes, the wells of gleaming blackness watching from another realm.

TOUCHING HER, PART TWO

Honolulu, 1868

During that first sojourn, now thirty years ago, I rented a cottage on the grounds of a new hotel, three rooms with coco palms overhead, flowering vines beside my porch, a splendid view across half an acre of well-tended lawn. Bits of blue ocean glinted through the farther line of trees, the kind of view, once you've savored it, once you've discovered that such a view can exist upon this Earth, you never want to leave. My windows were screened against insects but otherwise the whole place was open to the air, well ventilated by breezes flowing out of Nuʻuanu Valley, an ideal spot to pursue my triple task.

It was a short walk to the harbor and the gathering of ships I was ostensibly there to inspect, perhaps to buy. I knew a bit about this, having gone to sea for two years when I was seventeen, sailed our Atlantic coast from Florida to Newfoundland, across to Europe, to London, Gibraltar and Marseilles, before taking a post with my uncle's trading company. He was a farsighted fellow who'd sent me in search of three or four small vessels that might make regular runs from Honolulu to San Francisco. "The routes of trade," he said before I left, "will never be the same again."

He referred to the transcontinental railroad, about to be completed, which would link our coast to the Far West. He knew the months it took to bring a vessel around Cape Horn would soon be reduced to weeks, as goods began to flow both ways through San Francisco Bay—by rail, toward our eastern cities, as well as farther west, toward the numerous Pacific and Asian ports.

Shopping for ships, however, was the lesser task. It was a ruse, devised by this imaginative uncle of mine, to cover a much less public search. For certain politicians the completion of the railroad and the promise of expanded trade had given the islands new significance, rekindling an old desire to possess them and establish a base out there halfway across the ocean. Theirs was an oceanic vision, and Pearl Harbor was its centerpiece.

In those days, a year before the nailing of the famous Golden Spike at Promontory, Utah, joining the tracks that would span the continent, few eyes had yet viewed this harbor as a desirable U.S. holding. But my shrewd old uncle had joined forces with another farsighted colleague, a former classmate at Yale, then a congressman on the House Foreign Relations Committee, and very much in favor of joining Hawai'i to the United States. He'd studied the maps and shared a great curiosity about the land around the borders of that faraway lagoon. If some acreage were available, and if the price were right, the congressman would be a silent partner in a bit of long-range speculating. In the meantime he would advance the cause of annexation among his fellow committee members.

Once they learned that an assignment from the *Transcript* was taking me out that way, I was enlisted to do some poking around, make some discreet inquiries, etc., etc. "Take your time, son," said my uncle, his avuncular hand upon my shoulder. "And mind you now, keep your own counsel. That is, no need to advertise your intentions. If people over there find out what you're looking at, it could give them ideas they might not ordinarily have."

I traveled by train as far as Denver, then by stagecoach into California, and not once did it occur to me that I would be playing any part, even the very smallest part, in the fate of what seemed to me an improbably remote archipelago. I was too innocent to see that buying up some undervalued acreage beside a placid fishing lagoon could bring Hawai'i one step closer to America, its staunchest ally, its greatest threat. I had come of age in an era when all of this continent was seen as ours for the taking. By osmosis, that idea becomes part of you, the grand calling they have dubbed Manifest Destiny. Now that the Far West was ours, should the Pacific not be next? In our march from coast to coast, tribe after tribe had been uprooted, hunted down, shunted off to reservations, overrun by the same conquesting spirit that now yearned for the next great harbor, named for the pearl-bearing oysters clinging to its reefs.

If my voice sounds too strident here, taking on a kind of

pulpit zeal, perhaps it's a way of chastising myself, overdoing it in order to make up for past sins of my own. When I look back, how painfully clear it is that I too, like so many others, had reached the islands with scales on my eyes, afflicted, you might say, with an inherited type of foreigner's blindness.

Meanwhile, with naïve enthusiasm, I would send off my pieces to the Boston paper, personal, chatty, whatever came to mind. The editors gave me plenty of room, so long as I shed some light on what they and most of their readers saw as an exotic province of New England. In my first dispatch I had tried to describe that magical night on the deck (though I mentioned no names):

> Last Saturday it was my good fortune to attend a party on board the French frigate "Venus," recently arrived at the port. Civic leaders had been invited, both Hawaiian and white, intermingling with a remarkable familiarity, due in part, it seems to me, to the perpetual summer here. At twilight the air has a soothing, breezy voice that literally summons you forth. On my way to the harbor I passed native women clad in loose and flowing gowns, their heads encircled with garlands of fresh flowers, as they dashed along the main streets of the town seated man-fashion on their ponies…

* * *

Two weeks later I met Lydia Dominis for the second time, again thanks to my cousin Randall, who'd taken me under his wing in a brotherly way. A few years older and well connected in trading and shipping, he'd brought me into his circle. As I've mentioned, his wife, Lehua, the half-Hawaiian daughter of a prosperous Scotsman, had grown up with Lydia. One afternoon they invited me to join them on an excursion into the countryside, to the district called Waikiki, to see a house she'd recently occupied on some property that had been in her family for centuries.

"You really need to see that part of the island, Julius. There's nowhere else quite like it. All I ask is that you keep it to yourself."

"To myself?"

With a wink he said, "Don't write about this for the good burghers back home. It's one of our carefully guarded secrets."

These two made quite a striking couple, by the way. Randall was a robust, athletic fellow, a hiker and swimmer, who still had about him a youthful and collegiate air, the piercing blue eyes, the full head of hair parted in the middle, the wide brush of a moustache filling all the space between his upper lip and his Aryan nose. Lehua was a mixed-blood beauty, theatrically glamorous, slim-waisted, with glossy hair past her shoulders and burnished skin the hue of cocoa butter. It was odd, to say the least, having such a female "in the family." This was the first day we'd met. I confess that as we rode along I regarded the two of them with wonder, trying to imagine what their days were like together, not their public days, but the time spent alone, their nights and early mornings. Seeing them side by side, the archetypal Caucasian and the half-Hawaiian, I couldn't help but try to imagine them as lovers, her limbs and skin against his, all the while trying mightily not to imagine this, the thought itself a kind of violation of some forbidden zone.

At two o'clock we set out from the hotel grounds on horseback and quickly left the town behind. Honolulu had grown up beside the harbor, the wharves and warehouses, the steepled churches, white cottages, streets of crushed coral, flat and white as salt under sprawling, laden branches of flame tree and banyan. Waikiki lay some three miles south and west, connected to the town by a hard-packed dirt road that clung to the shoreline, much of it passing through groves of coco palms, high-tufted gray trunks lining each side like royal colonnades. Landed families, both Hawaiian and white, kept houses out there. Not far from the beach, freshwater streams fed into natural ponds, a haven for ducks. Farther inland, broad silver ponds were heavy with taro, the potato-like staple of the native diet. As an outer limit of Waikiki the long, furrowed crater and mariner's landmark called Diamond Head stood against a cloudless azure sky.

We were almost there when Randall eased his mount in next to mine. "I should tell you that this place came available to her just in time."

"In time for what?"

"We all know they've been having a rocky go of it."

"Randall! What a thing to say!"

Lehua's dark eyes glared at him. "Don't listen, Julius, don't listen to anything he says. That's just gossip." She wagged her head with a disapproving laugh. "You know how people talk."

"It isn't gossip, dear one. Everybody wonders what she's

doing out here by herself, and Julius will no doubt be wondering too."

She said nothing more, her interruption only half-hearted. I already knew that neither of them cared much for John Dominis, who was too full of himself, they'd said, having by that time risen to be Governor of the Island of Oahu, a largely ceremonial post but one he savored.

We rode in silence until Randall spoke again. "The sad truth is they're keeping separate houses now. Lydia probably won't mention this, but it weighs upon her, and she looks forward to callers."

Her house fronted on an open beach, not far from the crater. Rambling, unobtrusive, close to the ground, it was called *Paoakalani* (Heavenly Fragrance), for the many tropical flowers that filled the gardens.

As we tethered the horses we heard piano notes from somewhere inside, not a tune being played in tempo but clusters of notes, a single chord, a plink played again and again, tentative, searching. On the porch Lehua said, "She's working on another song."

I said, "Does she mind being interrupted?"

"She's always working on a song." Through the screen door she called, "Hooo-eee." And again, "Hooo-eee."

The tinkling stopped. "Hooo-eee," Lydia called back. *"Komo mai! Komo mai!"* (Come in! Come in!)

She met us in the shaded entryway, wearing one of those neck-to-ankle Mother Hubbard dresses Hawaiians call *muumuu*. Her eyes warm with welcome, she embraced them, pressing nose to nose.

Randall said, "You may remember my cousin, from Boston."

"Oh yes."

"On the night of the Frenchman's party, you danced with him."

"Of course, of course. And what a wonderful night that was."

Whether or not she remembered me I couldn't tell. Indeed she'd danced with so many men, and now two weeks had passed, surely it was all a blur. But if I was family to her good friends, then I too deserved a Polynesian embrace. She stepped toward me, pressing her nose to mine. With a voice as soft as velvet she murmured, "Aloha."

Though her cheek was soft as velvet too, it sparked an electric shock. I'd never been touched this way by any woman but my mother, yet this was not motherly, her voice almost a whisper.

"Welcome to my home," she said, ushering us into a spacious living room where rattan furniture was heaped with afghans and embroidered pillows. *"Komo mai, komo mai."*

Her piano was there, the centerpiece, a baby grand with composition pages scattered across the lid and spread along the music shelf above the keyboard. Nearby an autoharp leaned against the wall beside a music stand, and on the floor a guitar in its wooden case. It was a comfortably cluttered room, where Victorian bric-a-brac mingled with family treasures, a gourd drum, a dog's-tooth necklace, a darkly polished *koa* bowl, all cooled by ocean breezes drifting through screened windows that looked out onto her lanai.

She had some fruit punch waiting. As we settled in around it, she asked what had brought me to the islands and how long I'd be staying.

"Another month at least. Perhaps longer, now that I'm here."

"Hawai'i has had an effect on you."

"An enormous effect, yes."

With a tender glance at Randall she said, "You would not be the first to come here and change your plans."

"I certainly didn't expect it."

"So you're finding enough to write about, here in the uneventful tropics?"

"More than enough."

She nodded, nearly smiling, regarding me for a moment longer, as if this were all she needed to hear, or cared to hear, turning to Lehua, next to her on the rattan settee, who said that she loved the house, was so glad to see it at last, and what a blessing to be this close to the water.

Yes, said Lydia, she was happy here, supremely happy, with all her furniture finally in place. It had taken a month but it was worth the wait. She'd never before had a house of her own and had no idea what this was like. To come and go as one pleased, to sit down at the keyboard whenever she took a mind. She flung wide her arms, as if to say, 'Look around!,' her eyes ashine yet tinged with an edge of melancholy she couldn't conceal.

Lehua laid a sympathetic hand upon her arm, the childhood friend, sleek and stunning. Lydia was a fleshier woman, not heavy but fuller in the arms and in the bosom, with a fuller face, her skin somewhat darker, olive-hued, and black brows thicker. Compared with Lehua, she had a plainer look, and yet another beauty emanated from within, rising to the surface like the living glow in the dark *koa* bowl across the room, her glance by turns pensive, charming, stately. As the daughter of a high chief she possessed a compelling dignity that was already regal.

Lehua asked about the song she was working on, and at first Lydia demurred, said it was far from finished. But she was obviously glad to talk about it. They were both relieved that no more needed to be said (at least not then, not that afternoon, in the presence of a stranger) about whatever may have restricted her comings and goings in the household she'd left behind, relieved to be talking instead about a new song. Randall only had to ask if she'd play it for us and Lydia was moving toward the piano.

"No one has heard this. You will be the first."

The pages in front of her were busy with half notes and quarter notes penciled in among the clefs—a work in progress. Words had been crossed out and the title changed.

"Paia Ka Nahele," she explained to me, "means 'The Fragrant Forest.'"

From the first chords I could see she was accomplished and confident, her fingers supple on the keys. Her voice flowed without effort, an angelic voice, punctuated from time to time with a breaking note almost like a sob. I tried to imagine that fragrant forest, wondered what might have happened there, what lover's tryst, or broken promise, or bittersweet goodbye. Though the lyrics went untranslated, it didn't matter, the words but a conduit for this penetrating voice, both poignant and joyful, part lament, part celebration. And as she sang, I watched a veil fall away. As if freed from some old obligation, her body relaxed and her regal manner fell away.

With her final notes we three applauded, Randall and Lehua calling out, *"Hana hou! Hana hou!"* (Encore! Play some more!)

Flushed with the success of this little debut, basking in it, like a poet who has tried out a new ode, she played another, and this time I heard something else, a gospel quality, the congregational undertone. Before long I would learn that her training had started there, just as mine had, in the Sunday morning pews of her childhood. We knew all the same devotional songs, taken from pages of the same hymnal. But I also heard another note, something older and on that day still unfamiliar to me. I now know it was an echo of the chant tradition she'd been born into, from the time before missionaries brought their songs and brought writing to the islands, when all the prayers and invocations were spoken by low-throated chanters who kept alive the stories of famous deeds and demigods, when poems and love songs were chanted too. Lydia was of a generation that straddled the old time and the new. On that afternoon in her parlor I first heard it, a voice shaped in equal parts by Protestant harmonies and the chanter's haunting call.

This song too was greeted with demands for an encore. But she said no, she wanted to hear from her dearest friend, reaching low to lift the guitar from its case. Lehua too was eager to sing. She tried the strings to test the tuning, cranked one peg a tiny notch, and strummed a few simple chords, as more Hawaiian lyrics filled the room, her sweet voice in a higher range, with the clarity of a forest bird's. I began to understand that in Hawai'i singing is another way of talking, and sooner or later every social occasion turns musical.

After two songs with many verses, she tried to pass the guitar to Randall, but he preferred the piano, insisting that all of us join in, opening with a flourish, a long arpeggio up and down the keyboard, overdoing it, having some fun. The song was an old favorite they'd obviously sung before, the women's voices gathering around his sturdy tenor. Lydia took an alto line, Lehua sang lead:

Drink to me only with thine eyes
And I will pledge with mine,
Or leave a kiss but in the cup
And I'll not look for wine...

Needless to say, I knew this song. Who doesn't? In our family, when I was growing up, we'd sung it a hundred, perhaps a thousand times. One year at school, it was in the glee club's repertoire. My voice had dropped and suddenly I found myself standing among the baritones. Now I began to hum along, and by the second verse I was singing softly, in the lower register:

I sent thee late a rosey wreath,
Not so much honoring thee
As giving it a hope that there
It could not withered be...

Randall stopped playing.

"Julius! Julius! Come over here! Stand closer. I want to hear that bottom line. It's exactly what we need."

"By all means," said Lydia. "Let's do it again. I think we're going to have a real quartet!"

This time his arpeggio was even more theatrical, gleefully exaggerated. The volume of our combined voices seemed to double as we sang it through twice, four parts meshing as if we'd rehearsed for weeks.

We all congratulated ourselves, and now Lydia was regarding me as if for the first time, as if she'd been expecting me and I'd finally walked through the door.

"Maybe you have a song you would like to sing."

It was a gracious offer, a form of hospitality, accompanied by a playful glint that took me back to the frigate's deck, wondering again if she remembered that night and my desperate version of the waltz. Though singing, for me, is easier than dancing, I have never been much of a performer, not one to sing solo. I could have declined, of course, but an expectation hung in the humid, breezy atmosphere of her living room. Julius was next.

I'd known it would come to this, and I suppose I'd known there was no escape. At the side of my mind I'd been sorting through titles. In Boston a new song had been making the rounds, heard in taverns and music halls. I asked Randall if he knew it, and yes, maybe once, somewhere, he'd heard it sung. Lydia had heard the title, which intrigued her. No circus had ever found its way to Honolulu, she'd never seen a trapeze, but she'd seen photos of the moustachioed acrobats in their tights and doublets.

Randall was blessed with a good ear. I had only to hum the melody once and he found the key and the chords. Like a cabaret dandy I took my place beside the baby grand, one hand flat upon its gleaming lid.

Oh, he'd fly through the air
With the greatest of ease,

The daring young man on the flying trapeze.
His movements were graceful,
All girls he would please,
And my love he has stolen away…

I knew four verses and sang them with all the gusto at my command, spurring Randall to flashy keyboard work that lifted me toward a rousing and burlesque finale, my head thrown back, one hand pressed against my heart like a dying Italian tenor.

"Bravo!" he cried.

"Yes, bravo," said Lydia, who wanted these lyrics for their repertoire, insisting that I copy them down so that next time we could all sing together about this daring young man.

What next time? I wondered. Had I passed some sort of test?

To find out, I would have to wait another hour. Randall and I followed with "Yankee Doodle." Lydia picked up her autoharp and the women sang another of her Hawaiian ballads, *"Nani Na Pua"* (Beautiful Flower). Then we all sang "Jeannie with the Light Brown Hair" and "The Bonny Banks of Loch Lomond." And so it went until the sun began to drop, when she remembered that we hadn't seen the other rooms or toured the garden. But that would have to wait for another day. Rain clouds loomed over the inland peaks. Randall wanted to get back before dark.

Soon we were outside on the verandah for our farewells. Almost as an afterthought, Lydia said sweetly, "You have sung in church."

"For many years."

"I can hear it in the way you harmonize."

"I can hear it in your voice too, if you don't mind my saying so."

"I wonder if you would care to join us sometime, a small group of like-minded people who enjoy making music…in a most informal way. Randall and Lehua can tell you about it as you ride."

"My goodness, yes! Of course. It would be my great privilege."

Those two now stepped down, heading for the horses. She waited a moment and said, "Well then…until we meet again. Aloha."

Her brief embrace and the way she spoke—the murmured and satiny softness—unnerved me. Two weeks in the islands and I was still uncertain about the nature of this word, which can mean so many things at once: Welcome. Hello. Goodbye. Until we meet. I miss you. I like you. I love you. I'd heard sailors throwing the word around as if Aloha were a bawdy joke. Among Hawaiians you never hear it used lightly, always uttered with care, with a warmth that is itself a kind of embrace meant to convey an unconditional generosity of spirit. But this had not yet come clear to me. Call it another feature of my blindness.

While Randall and Lehua stepped into the yard, Lydia's voice had dropped, as if we were alone in the hushed and sultry air of her garden, seeming to suggest another kind of invitation. There was no reason for me to hear it like that. She was, after all, a married woman, a Christian woman, eminently desirable in my eyes, yet in no way flirtatious. Indeed, she would never have allowed herself to be. Even so, she was vulnerable for reasons entirely new to her, separated from John Dominis after seven years, and living alone three miles from town.

As I would soon learn from Randall, she'd never won over the mother-in-law, who resented her as she would have resented any woman who might try to claim some part of her son's affection. And Dominis, alas, lacked the will to stand up to his mother. For seven years, in her husband's home, Lydia had been made to feel like a second-class citizen.

For a woman of the chiefly class it wasn't unusual to have her own quarters, to manage her own land, if she had some. As soon as Paoakalani came available she moved to Waikiki, assuming that John would join her there, hoping he'd seize the chance to break away at last. But he didn't—a final signal that he actually preferred his mother's company. At that point I think Lydia gave up on him. It seems to me now, thinking back, that they gave up on each other. They'd had no children. For reasons that still elude me, they stayed married, living apart, for another twenty years, until the mother finally passed away.

Before I left Honolulu that year I would meet John Dominis at a large banquet hosted by the king, a glittering affair with champagne beforehand and an abundant table, from which Dominis excused himself about halfway through the meal, saying he wasn't feeling well. Something about his back, he muttered to those of us within range of his chair. This was how—she would tell me later—he escaped any situation that didn't suit him. The sudden ailment. The chronic affliction. Much like his mother, said Lydia, who believed this habit ran in their family. Ailments of convenience.

At that first meeting I could see it in his smile—I should say, in his effort not to smile. He was a slim and dour man whose mouth and chin and neck were nearly covered by a dark, well-cultivated beard. "My jaws," his muffled lips seemed to imply, "they cannot bear too much activity, so forgive me if I restrain myself."

Reluctant to smile or to offer much else, he nodded stiffly, made his early exit, and I wouldn't see him again for twenty years. So I can't honestly say I knew the man. And yet, in a sort of tribal way, I felt I did. We were, after all, of similar stock, his origins much like my own, his mother, like mine, from a longtime Boston family. He too was educated there, attending the same school as his prosperous cousin, William Lee—until they carried him off to Honolulu, where, as luck and motherly ambition would have it, he found himself for a time enrolled in the same school as the girl he would eventually marry.

I'm going to hazard an opinion here—no, not as firm as that. Call it a speculation about her preference through the years for men from my part of the country. It started with that school's headmaster, a man from the missionary generation, a rigid disciplinarian, sometimes accused of being too ready to punish, too handy with the rod and the ruler, yet an apt teacher who introduced Lydia to the English language, to Western music and American history. She boarded there for several years, under the constant eye of this early mentor from Danbury, Connecticut, who first opened her eyes and ears to the sounds and stories of a land she would later have to understand, whether she wanted to or not. I think again of the man chosen to preside at her wedding, "The Seaman's Friend," from Holden, Massachusetts, educated at Amherst and Andover Theological Seminary. The man she chose to marry that day was born in Boston, as was the man she would choose to deliver her private mail and answer most of it, compose her press releases, and travel with her through the winter and into the spring of 1897. And I don't mean this to sound self-serving. This is merely speculation, but with my thirty years of hindsight it seems to me that for Lydia Dominis, fated to be a queen, there was some inherent, even perverse affinity for men from the northeast corner of the United States. You might call it an odd and inevitable tribute to the many lessons and sermons of those gospel-bearing moralizers who, from before she was born, were already reshaping her island world.

⋆ ⋆ ⋆

A week later an envelope appeared in my box at the hotel, her name engraved in indigo ink in the upper left-hand corner. Inside, on blue-bordered stationery, the handwritten message said,

> Please join us at Paoakalani for an afternoon of music and good companionship. Saturday, the 18th of February at 3 p.m. A light meal will be served. With my Aloha, LYDIA DOMINIS

It was the first of several invitations to sing-alongs and soirees at her Waikiki retreat. Randall and Lehua were always there, and Lydia's companion/retainer who sometimes spent a weekend, and a cheerful young Hawaiian fellow who sang falsetto and played the fiddle—five or ten or a dozen people who shared her love for food and music.

"A light meal," as it turned out, was a ridiculous understatement. "Hawaiians don't eat until we're full," she once confided. "We eat until we're tired."

We each brought a potluck contribution, some fruit, some poi, some coconut pudding. After two or three hours of music-making, an elaborate spread of dishes would be laid out on mats, luau-style, where we ate and talked about food, about Hawaiian songs and American songs and the price of sugar on the American market, about Honolulu politics and the royal family, and—if we lingered into the evening—in the dim light of a whale-oil lantern we'd consider the prophetic meaning of recent nature signs, a sudden storm, a double rainbow, the appearance of an owl or a shark or a wild pig, a new show of lava on the Big Island far to the south.

Lydia was fond of Hawaiian proverbs. "One can think about life after the fish is in the canoe," she would say. "And what does that mean? Well, for us the fish is the singing of our songs. And now, for today, we have put that fish into its canoe, so we can think about anything we like."

On one such afternoon, as we lounged about her living room, an exquisite light surrounded us, a lemony light tinged with silver, coming through her windows from the west. The sun was close to the horizon, and she announced that we should all walk out to the water's edge and watch what happens to the sky. Barefooted she led the way as we trudged across the sand and plopped down just where the farthest lick of an inrolling tide left its frothy edge.

I managed to place myself next to her, a bit closer than I'd intended, but she didn't mind. Under the ample skirts of her Mother Hubbard she carefully crossed her legs, folded her hands in her lap, as if this were a frequent ritual. For quite some time we sat in silence, watching a cluster of puffy clouds turn from lemon to tangerine, and above the clouds a quality of blue I'd seen nowhere else, a soothing and gentler blue backlit by a falling sun and laced with silver. It lit our faces and lit the famous landmark off to our left, of which Lydia now began to speak in her softest voice, evidently meant for me alone, since all our voices there were muffled by the sea. With water lapping close to shore and low swells breaking farther out, a steady rush surrounded us. I had to cup my ear and lean in close.

"Many years ago, they say, a British ship came around the point, as they all do, bound for Honolulu harbor, and the sailors on board saw some glints on the side of the crater. They thought they were diamonds embedded in the slope, just there for the taking. Once their ship dropped anchor they hurried back out here and climbed the slope hoping to gather up their treasure. Imagine their disappointment when they learned that the glints came not from diamonds but from shiny stones scattered among the rocks that once were lava. Even though there were no diamonds, that is the name that all travelers use today. Those sailors didn't know that the rocks and shiny stones offered something much more precious. Old volcanoes made the very land we live on. I think it tells us something about a great many visitors to our islands. They arrive by ship and think they have found some special treasure that is theirs to keep and they fail to see what is really here."

She turned to me then, reaching across to touch my

arm, her face half-lit by the orange sky. "But I have to say, Julius, not every visitor is like that."

Her touch was a burning match upon my skin. Her story had seared me, like a scolding. I felt her words were aimed at me, as if she knew of our scheme or perhaps had come to accept that every foreigner, whether American or British or Spanish or French, had something up the sleeve. She and I had visited Pearl Harbor, a daylong outing on horseback, a half dozen of us with mats and baskets, for a picnic on a shady point. They'd all heard rumors of America's interest in that vast lagoon and agreed it would be a bad idea to cede control of any part of the kingdom to another nation. It is a wondrous body of water, serenely tranquil, with verdant mountains to the east and west. While little was said of the surrounding terrain that day, the empty shoreline that curves for miles, my silent and calculating survey may have given me away. This was my fear, as Lydia and I sat side by side in the sand at sundown: she already knew that much about me.

Her voice was tender. Her smile was sweet. Her eyes had the ancestral look. For a split second I saw two women there, one who'd played and sung and dined with such delight, and some elder, a great-great-grandmother, a chanter and healer and seer who'd rejoined us from some older time, a hundred and fifty years ago.

"There are those," she went on, "who listen before they speak, who finally see who we are."

This did not describe me in those days. Yet instantly I knew it was someone I must learn to be. And in that same moment I saw that I could no longer play a part in my uncle's game. I'd seen enough, heard enough to know that money could be made—in the long run quite a bit of money. I wanted none of it. But how to divest myself? How to dissuade him from proceeding?

As if by telegraph, a letter began to pass through my mind, sentences unfolding, one upon the next. I could see the words. Don't bother with Pearl Harbor, I would say, you'll only be wasting capital...Would he believe me? Probably not. I would send it anyway. I was a young man then. I still believed that virtue could prevail.

I fell backward onto the sand, suddenly weightless. An anvil had been lifted from my shoulders, a burden I'd been unaware of until it floated away.

She looked down at me, amused. "Are you all right?"

"Never better. It's glorious out here!"

"The best part of the day."

"You say Diamond Head describes something that isn't there."

"Yes."

"And had never been there."

"Yes."

"What then is the Hawaiian name?"

As if waiting for this question, she said, "It is *Leahi,* the brow of the tuna. You can see why, from the brow of the crater's peak. A much better name, don't you think, for a crater that has come rising from the sea? Tuna are swimming out there right now, where the lava used to flow."

As I sat up, a dark figure appeared in the molten sea, with the contours of a large fish caught in the swell of a rising wave. Then it lifted, as if to stand upon the water, and a man was on his feet, standing on a narrow plank, gliding toward shore, seemingly without effort, arms at his sides, until the long wave played itself out. He dropped to his knees, dipped his arms into the surge and began paddling. We watched until he stood in the shallows, hoisted the dark board on top of his head and walked off down the beach.

"Amazing," I said, "truly amazing. I see them down by the harbor, every morning very early the young men are out there."

"We all love the water. In our family my father taught us how. He was quite famous, you know, as a surfrider."

"You too can ride the waves?"

"Not the big ones. But yes, I keep a board beside the house."

"I hear only Hawaiians can do it. *Haoles* never get the knack."

"This is what they say."

"I wonder if it's true."

"Can you swim?"

"During my years at sea I learned to swim quite well."

Her mouth curved into its playful smile, as if preparing to say something that might startle me. But the sky interrupted her. The tangerine-tinted cloud cover had exploded into a fiery panorama. From the horizon to the flames right overhead, the heavens were ablaze, one of those moments when you can't speak, shouldn't speak. We sat and let the colors cover us, red and orange streaked with violet, flooding that entire district called Waikiki. On such an evening, is there any lovelier spot on earth? Such drama in the water, with lines of surf lifting through the glossy textures of the bay, tinted by the skies above, the white fringe rushing shoreward—all presided over by the majestic promontory the Hawaiians call Leahi.

In my memory that sundown is the image for a blessed terrain they had long inhabited in total isolation, not a perfect people, by any measure—indeed, who of us can claim to be?—but a people with their own ways of being human, in an archipelago for so many centuries self-sufficient and self-contained. It has been both their blessing and their curse to have found a homeland the rest of the world simply cannot leave alone, too delicious, too lovely, too well placed in the shipping lanes. But as of that evening in 1868, Lydia Dominis still had this house named for heavenly fragrance, on land passed down to her from a grandfather born before the ships of Captain Cook arrived. Whatever had gone wrong between her and the man she married, she still possessed this unobstructed view of a setting sun that can fill the eyes and the heart with an inspirational fire.

AFTERWORD

Maxine Hong Kingston

The setting sun filling our eyes and our hearts with inspirational fire, the story can well end. Jim Houston has finished the tale, satisfying and whole. He made time flash back just enough so that we know how Queen Lili'uokalani came to be abroad on an open-ended journey. The Americans have taken Hawai'i. Narrator Julius Palmer envisions the book he wants to write: "...a full-length study of modern-day Hawai'i and how its fate bears upon our national agenda, this mad dream of an American empire that reaches so far beyond our natural borders and halfway across to Asia." The sun sets on the *'aina*.

And yet, there are openings for more story. Will the queen sail for England to plot with Princess Kai'ulani? Who is making the death threats? Will there be an attempt on the queen's life? Will the would-be assassins be caught? What of the book the queen is writing? So far she has "only notes, only notes."

Recall the scene where Lili'uokalani pardons President Cleveland with a large forgiveness for his transgressions: "She possessed that quality," says Julius, "as if offering a kind of papal absolution. She could also pronounce a curse that would one day make my scalp crawl." Jim Houston, a born writer, must have looked forward with relish to writing the scene about the day the queen throws her curse. Her voice, resonant with the voices of the ancestors and the music of the *'aina,* and *aloha,* would explode like wrathful diety Madam Pele's. What words did she spew forth? What was the ultimate provocation? Who received the curse, and what awfulness befell?

In *Hawaii's Story by Hawaii's Queen*—she did finish writing the book in Boston, and had it published there, in 1898—Lili'uokalani warned "honest Americans" and "Christians" to "not covet the little vineyard of Naboth's so far from your shores, lest the punishment of Ahab fall upon you, if not in your day, in that of your children, for 'be not deceived, God is not mocked.'" The curse against Ahab, taker of Naboth's vineyard, goes as follows: "Thus saith the Lord, in the place where dogs licked the blood of Naboth shall dogs lick thy blood, even thine." There are families in Hawai'i to this day who believe that their misfortunes have been brought upon them by the queen's curse.

If Jim Houston had lived to write Part Two of *A Queen's Journey,* he would have written her diary—continued the diary that disappeared when she was arrested. We'd know Lili'uokalani's secret thoughts and feelings. We'd find out about her lovers. We'd see the romance with Julius from her point of view. Julius told about it with the discretion of a descendant of Puritans. The queen would write sexily, like *hula kolili,* the dance with love forfeits.

Queen Liliʻuokalani was a prodigious writer, putting a civilization into words as it was being annihilated. *Hawaii's Story by Hawaii's Queen* made every argument against takeover by the United States. She translated into English the *Kumulipo,* the Hawaiian creation chant. She composed over two hundred songs, including the Hawaiian national anthem and the farewell song "Aloha Oe." Writing in her diary was an ongoing habit.

Jim Houston could have channeled her voice. He'd trained his writer's ear to hear the voices of women. He could write from their point of view—as Jeanne Wakatsuki Houston, his wife and collaborator on *Farewell to Manzanar;* as Holly Doyle in *Love Life;* as Patty Reed in *Snow Mountain Passage;* and as the diarist mother in *Bird of Another Heaven.* Completed, *A Queen's Journey* would've been his masterpiece, a love story told half by the man, half by the woman, a perfectly matching pair.

AUTHOR BIOS

JAMES D. HOUSTON was born in San Francisco and received his master's degree in American literature from Stanford, where he studied under Wallace Stegner, Irving Howe, and Frank O'Connor. Long considered a literary master of the West, Houston authored eight books, including *Bird of Another Heaven, Snow Mountain Passage, Farewell to Manzanar,* and *Where Light Takes Its Color from the Sea: A California Notebook*. His stories and essays have been widely anthologized and earned numerous honors. In 1962 he moved with his wife, Jeanne Wakatsuki Houston, into an old Victorian house in Santa Cruz and taught writing at the nearby University of California for over twenty years while dividing his time between California and Hawai'i.

ALAN CHEUSE is the author of four novels, three collections of short fiction, and the memoir *Fall Out of Heaven*. He is a regular contributor to National Public Radio's "All Things Considered," and his short fiction has appeared in *The New Yorker, Ploughshares, The Antioch Review, Prairie Schooner, New Letters, The Idaho Review,* and *The Southern Review.* He teaches in the writing program at George Mason University and at the Squaw Valley Community of Writers. His website is www.alancheuse.com.

MAXINE HONG KINGSTON is the National Book Award–winning author of *China Men, The Woman Warrior, Tripmaster Monkey, The Fifth Book of Peace,* and, most recently, a memoir-in-poems, *I Love a Broad Margin to My Life.* She is a professor emeritus of English at the University of California, Berkeley, and she lives in Oakland.

Heyday Announces the James D. Houston Legacy Fund

> "If there is one California-grown, longtime California writer who seems to be changing things, it is James D. Houston." —Alan Cheuse

Friends and family of Santa Cruz author James D. Houston have established a fund to honor his memory and further his legacy. Known as a masterful writer in both fiction and nonfiction genres, Jim Houston was also a dedicated teacher and passionate promoter of emerging authors. The James D. Houston Legacy Fund supports publication of books by writers who reflect Jim's humane values, his thoughtful engagement with life, and his literary exploration of California, Hawai'i, and the West. Books sponsored by the fund, while of the highest literary quality, are those unable to support themselves on earned income alone.

The James D. Houston Fund is administered by Heyday, a 501(c)(3) nonprofit publisher much admired by Jim. Nominations and decisions as to which writers to support are made collegially by Heyday's publisher, Malcolm Margolin; by the Houston family, represented by Jim's wife, Jeanne Wakatsuki Houston; and by friends of the late author. Heyday will publish, distribute, and promote the books selected and is committed to matching donations on a dollar-to-dollar basis from funds of its own.

Jim was a person of great integrity, a meticulous craftsman, a devoted teacher, and a generous friend. Jim graced the world with a warmth, intelligence, and vision that has left a profound mark on the literary culture of the West. We look forward to creating books through the James D. Houston Legacy Fund that will honor not just his literary skills but also the fullness of his being.

Donations (tax-deductible) to the James D. Houston Legacy Fund can be made by calling (510) 549-3564, ext. 304, or by sending a check made out to Heyday to the following address:

Heyday
c/o the James D. Houston Legacy Fund
P.O. Box 9145
Berkeley, California 94709

Those wishing to submit manuscripts for consideration, please refer to our guidelines at www.heydaybooks.com.

About Heyday

Heyday is an independent, nonprofit publisher and unique cultural institution. We promote widespread awareness and celebration of California's many cultures, landscapes, and boundary-breaking ideas. Through our well-crafted books, public events, and innovative outreach programs we are building a vibrant community of readers, writers, and thinkers.

Thank You

It takes the collective effort of many to create a thriving literary culture. We are thankful to all the thoughtful people we have the privilege to engage with. Cheers to our writers, artists, editors, storytellers, designers, printers, bookstores, critics, cultural organizations, readers, and book lovers everywhere!

We are especially grateful for the generous funding we've received for our publications and programs during the past year from foundations and hundreds of individual donors. Major supporters include:

Anonymous; James Baechle; Bay Tree Fund; B.C.W. Trust III; S. D. Bechtel, Jr. Foundation; Barbara Jean and Fred Berensmeier; Berkeley Civic Arts Program and Civic Arts Commission; Joan Berman; Peter and Mimi Buckley; Lewis and Sheana Butler; California Council for the Humanities; California Indian Heritage Center Foundation; California State Library; California Wildlife Foundation / California Oak Foundation; Keith Campbell Foundation; Candelaria Foundation; John and Nancy Cassidy Family Foundation, through Silicon Valley Community Foundation; The Christensen Fund; Compton Foundation; Lawrence Crooks; Nik Dehejia; George and Kathleen Diskant; Donald and Janice Elliott, in honor of David Elliott, through Silicon Valley Community Foundation; Federated Indians of Graton Rancheria; Mark and Tracy Ferron; Furthur Foundation; The Fred Gellert Family Foundation; Wallace Alexander Gerbode Foundation; Wanda Lee Graves and Stephen Duscha; Alice Guild; Walter & Elise Haas Fund; Coke and James Hallowell; Carla Hills; Sandra and Chuck Hobson; G. Scott Hong Charitable Trust; James Irvine Foundation; JiJi Foundation; Marty and Pamela Krasney; Guy Lampard and Suzanne Badenhoop; LEF Foundation; Judy McAfee; Michael McCone; Mary Philpotts McGrath; Joyce Milligan; Moore Family Foundation; National Endowment for the Arts; National Park Service; Theresa Park; Pease Family Fund, in honor of Bruce Kelley; The Philanthropic Collaborative; PhotoWings; Resources Legacy Fund; Alan Rosenus; Rosie the Riveter/WWII Home Front NHP; The San Francisco Foundation; San Manuel Band of Mission Indians; Savory Thymes; Hans Schoepflin; Contee and Maggie Seely; Stanley Smith Horticultural Trust; William Somerville; Judith Flanders Staub; Stone Soup Fresno; James B. Swinerton; Swinerton Family Fund; Thendara Foundation; Tides Foundation; TomKat Charitable Trust; Lisa Van Cleef and Mark Gunson; Whole Systems Foundation; John Wiley & Sons; Peter Booth Wiley and Valerie Barth; Dean Witter Foundation; and Yocha Dehe Wintun Nation.

Board of Directors

Getting Involved

To learn more about our publications, events, membership club, and other ways you can participate, please visit www.heydaybooks.com.

Heyday is committed to preserving ancient forests and natural resources. We elected to print this title on 30% post consumer recycled paper, processed chlorine free. As a result, for this printing, we have saved:

4 Trees (40' tall and 6-8" diameter)
1 Million BTUs of Total Energy
423 Pounds of Greenhouse Gases
1,909 Gallons of Wastewater
121 Pounds of Solid Waste

Heyday made this paper choice because our printer, Thomson-Shore, Inc., is a member of Green Press Initiative, a nonprofit program dedicated to supporting authors, publishers, and suppliers in their efforts to reduce their use of fiber obtained from endangered forests.

For more information, visit www.greenpressinitiative.org

Environmental impact estimates were made using the Environmental Defense Paper Calculator. For more information visit: www.papercalculator.org.